Peter Lancett is a writer, fiction editor and filmmaker, living and working in New Zealand and sometimes Los Angeles.

He claims that one day he'll settle down and get a proper job.

Seeing Red

PETER LANCETT

CUTTING EDGE

Breaking Dawn
DONNA SHELTON

The Finer Points of Becoming Machine
EMILY ANDREWS

Marty's Diary
FRANCES CROSS

The Only Brother
CAIAS WARD

The Questions Within
TERESA SCHAEFFER

Seeing Red
PETER LANCETT

© Ransom Publishing Ltd. 2008

This edition is published by arrangement with Ransom Publishing Ltd.

SADDLEBACK
EDUCATIONAL PUBLISHING
www.sdlback.com

© 2012 by Saddleback Educational Publishing

ISBN-13: 978-1-61651-759-5
ISBN-10: 1-61651-759-X

Printed in Guangzhou, China
0512/CA21200795

16 15 14 13 12   2 3 4 5 6 7

CHAPTER 1

My best friend's sister

I was out with Eddie last night. Eddie's my best friend, though I guess that's not saying much; I don't really *have* friends. Just a few people I say "hi" to now and then. I say "hi" to Eddie more often than anyone else and I suppose that makes him my best friend, but we're certainly not close in the way that you are with *your* best friend. Phew—I should have taken a breath there!

Anyway, like I was saying, I was out with Eddie last night. We're not doing much, just hanging around on the street corners. We kinda like it that people cross the streets to avoid us and nobody wants to look us in the eye. Just what they think we are or what we'll do I can't imagine. Well actually, I can; they think that we're going to vandalize the neighborhood and maybe trash their cars after dark when they're safe behind their curtains. Eddie wears a hoodie and never smiles when there are people around. He likes how that freaks them out. I like it too, if I'm honest. The thing is, you'd think that people would *know* that we're not out for trouble just by looking at *me*.

You see, while Eddie likes to think he's cool—he always wears the latest stuff—I don't go in for it. Even just hanging around on the streets with Eddie I'm wearing penny loafers by Prada and Ralph Lauren casual pants, a two-button jacket by Sean John and an open-collar Pierre Cardin shirt. And if other kids laugh at me and sneer—and they do—I take comfort in the knowledge that my shoes cost more than their entire wardrobes. In some cases, that would go for my haircut too. What? So I have parents who can afford it and like to indulge me. So what? Saves them ever having to listen to me.

So where was I? Oh, that's right; I'm hanging out with Eddie last night. We're sitting in the bus shelter across from the playground. Eddie is chain-smoking as he sometimes does. French cigarettes that give off an awful smell. We are waiting for his bus—Eddie lives a couple of miles away— and Eddie starts talking about girls. Eddie says that most people at school think that I'm queer because of the way I dress. As if I don't know *that* already.

"So are you?"

"Am I what?"

"You know… queer."

There, see. I told you we're not really close.

"Well, if it puts your mind at ease, no. No I'm not."

It crosses my mind that Eddie might not believe me. We sit in silence for a moment, with him drawing slowly on his cigarette while I wait in vain for him to erupt in spasms of uncontrolled coughing.

"Who do you like out of our class?"

A trail of vacant faces passes before me. The girls in our class. What a carnival. I won't describe them now; maybe later.

"None of them, really."

"Then you are queer. Not even Joanna Stevens?"

Actually I don't like Joanna Stevens, but that's because I've heard her speak. I can see where Eddie is coming from though. If it came down to just looks and nothing more than that, you'd have to hand it to Joanna Stevens. Even wearing nothing better than off-the-rack "mall chic" I have to admit that she is a superior class of slut.

"No, not even her. I've seen trees with more brains."

Eddie doesn't look at me. He blows a

My best friend's sister

long plume of blue-gray smoke out between his lips as he flips the glowing cigarette butt into the gutter.

"Brains? We're not talking about picking a debating team here!"

Eddie laughs and turns to me, smiling.

"Really though; wouldn't you just like to get her in the dark and run your hands all over her?"

I smile back and shake my head.

"No, no I wouldn't…" There is a pause. "Well, OK, maybe that does sound good. But then I'd have to speak to her the next day. It just wouldn't be worth it."

Eddie laughs and shoves me playfully.

"Oh it would be worth it all right, trust me. That's a small price to pay."

I raise my eyebrows quizzically.

"Trust me, it is. At least we know that you're not queer."

"I've always known."

Eddie looks at me.

"Go on then, who *do* you like?"

For a moment a face flickers at the front of my mind. A girl from school and she's in our grade but not in our class. I find myself looking at her whenever she's out and about at the same time that we are. I can't tell Eddie this though; word would get out, and that would mean hassle for me. And perhaps for this girl. She doesn't deserve that.

"There *is* somebody, I can tell."

Eddie. So perceptive he should be a hostage negotiator or a forensic psychiatrist for the FBI.

"Eddie, I can't tell you. It would be embarrassing."

"Only for you, jerk-off. Go on, who is it? Not that brainiac woman from that TV show is it? Well, is it?"

Eddie keeps pushing and pushing and he's joking and teasing but he won't stop. And another face comes to mind. Another girl I find attractive, no doubt about it. But this is forbidden fruit.

"No, it's not the woman from TV, Eddie. Christ, she must be a hundred years old!'

The woman is probably in her thirties but that's how we see her. It's the way we speak and we can't help it. Thirties is ancient to us. Then I realize what I've said, and Eddie is sharp enough to pick up on it too. His dad is a lawyer and some of that sharpness must have been passed down.

"So there is an *it*, a somebody. Come on, I won't tell anyone. And *you* know that *I'd* bite my own arm off to get my hands on Joanna Stevens. So tell."

"Hand."

Eddie looks puzzled.

"Hand. If you bite off an arm you'll only have one hand to get all over Joanna Stevens."

"Oh very smart... asshole! Now come on. Tell."

The face again—the forbidden face, not the girl from school, although this girl *does* go to our school—it's there floating past me. And not just the face, the whole package; a provocative teenage minx.

"Can't we just talk about something else?"

Stupid question, but I have to try.

"No, no we can't! Who is it? What do you want to do with her? Do you see yourself with her, getting jiggy? Do you imagine yourself with her and you're both really hot for each other?"

Eddie is on a roll and it's almost like I'm not there at all.

"What's it feel like when you have your hands inside her top, eh? Don't pretend you don't have these thoughts. We all do. Who is she? C'mon—you gotta tell. Perhaps I can set you up."

"It's Helen."

I say the words and realize what I've done and I know that I can't take them back and I so wish that I could but it's too late.

"See, that was easy. Helen..." Eddie is searching his mind's rolodex to find an appropriate Helen and he's struggling. I try to appear cool in the hope that he'll run out of ideas and it can remain my secret. I look down at my shoes.

"I only know one Helen. And I think we can count *her* out."

I'm still looking at my shoes and I can feel Eddie's eyes on me. The atmosphere has changed, just like that. I should smile and come back with a sharp remark; easy to say, but it's too late. I make matters worse by shrugging, and as I turn to Eddie to explain that's it's all innocent, I'm just in time to see the punch that Eddie's swinging. Instinctively I roll away and off the seat. Eddie still catches me though, and I feel a thud to my cheek, but there is no pain. Adrenaline I guess.

"My Helen? You just stay away from her, you dirty bastard!"

I'm rolling away and catch a hefty kick in the ribs, but I manage to get up and start running. It's only when I realize that I can't hear footsteps pounding after me that I stop and turn.

Eddie is not pursuing me and he's walking backwards towards the bus stop. He seems to be looking not at me but down the road beyond me, so that I turn to look too. Now I see why he is not racing after me. A bus is coming towards us. Eddie's bus.

"You're a filthy perv," Eddie shouts for all the world to hear. Thankfully the streets are deserted. "You just stay the hell away from Helen!"

The bus has swept past me. It is pulling up at the stop as Eddie points at me and makes a throat-slitting gesture with his fingers, before turning and boarding.

I catch my breath and shake my head as I watch the bus pull away. I've never seen Eddie turn like that. Obviously he was shocked to hear that I found Helen attractive. But she is a fox, and she knows it too, and surely Eddie can see it.

And I can't believe that Eddie would attack me like that, no matter what. It's not like *I'd* been talking about getting my hands all over her—those were Eddie's own words, not mine, and Eddie's thoughts too, come to that, not mine. What did he mean, calling me a perv? It's not like I'm some kind of pedophile is it? So what if I'm sixteen and Helen is thirteen? If I was twenty-five and she was twenty-two, would it matter to anyone? And anyway, *I* never said I wanted to do *anything* with her, anything at all.

I wonder if Eddie is still my best friend? After all, it's not my fault that Eddie has a really hot kid sister.

CHAPTER 2

Looking sharp, Tom

I don't have a black eye, and that's amazing. I'm looking in the bathroom mirror. It's morning and the cheekbone under my left eye is a little swollen and a little red. But there's no bruising. I doubt that anyone would ever notice. I'm guessing that *I* only notice because I'm so familiar with my own face. It hurts though. Not a raging pain, just a presence. It sits like a coiled snake, waiting to strike, waiting for a wrong move. So I make the wrong move by poking at it. The pain is immediate, spreads all down my face and even spills out into my shoulder. And although it's pain, it's strangely addictive so that I can't help poking it a couple of times more. It's like how you can't help poking a canker sore with the tip of your tongue. Like that, but much more intense.

There *is* a bruise on my ribs though. It's blue in the middle and red at the edges. It doesn't hurt at all until I move. Then I feel it, sharp and shrill. I'll just have to live with it, I guess, until it fades away. I certainly don't have any desire to poke at it, that's for sure.

A banging at the bathroom door. Every morning it's the same.

"Are you finished in there? *Come on, I'm gonna be late!*"

I *so* want to tell you that the voice is harsh and obnoxious, but you can hear it for yourself and clearly that is not the case. The diction is perfect, disguising even the tiny lapse into slang. And the sounds are sweet. Like the tinkling of angel bells or the lazy babbling of a gentle brook. Not that I'd ever tell Madeleine any of this; she has a high enough opinion of herself already, does my darling sister.

No, really; she is a darling. And I love her to bits, even if she is three years older than me and we sometimes find ourselves squabbling. There's quite a bond between us, to tell the truth. We just do a good job of disguising it sometimes.

"Mom—"

Here we go again...

"Tom's hogging the bathroom and I'm gonna be late!"

Late for what, I wonder? But this is a ritual, so I check on the towel around my waist and open the door ready to play my part.

Madeleine is standing just beyond the frame. She's wearing these great pajamas— Tiffany Blues from Bedhead—and her blonde hair is only slightly disheveled. It's still obvious why boys are always swarming around her.

"God, what's happened to you?"

No ritual banter this morning then. I brush past her.

"Nice PJs."

I don't look back but I know that she'll be glowing inside from the compliment. For Madeleine, nothing on earth is more important than fashion. She's the reason that I like fine clothes myself. I guess you could say that she trained me. Over the years, I'd hate to guess how many hours I've spent in her room, watching her try on clothes. And no, I don't actually watch her getting dressed and undressed, sicko; she has a walk-in. My job is always to say what I think goes and what doesn't. I'd have to say that Madeleine has trained me well, because I do have a very good eye. I really do.

You might wonder why Mom doesn't spend this kind of time with Madeleine. Well, you should know that Mom and Dad are the kind of people who only had kids to complete the picture. Successful careers—check. Great house in the suburbs—check. Mercedes and BMW in the garage—check.

Two beautiful, trouble-free kids—check. At least, that's what I think. And yeah, come on; just look at us. We're beautiful all right.

We are not neglected or mistreated—far from it. There's always been money. And Madeleine and I have always been able to indulge our love of fashion. But what we've never had tons of is time and attention. We're not alone in this, I know, and I'm not whining. I just want you to know that while our relationship with our parents is not exactly sterile, Madeleine and I have always turned to each other for comfort and advice.

So I'm not surprised that Madeleine notices the redness on my face. She's bound to, really. Still, I very much doubt that anyone else will.

Walking downstairs, I'm dressed and feeling cool and confident. Clothes can do that for me. It's like I'm a different person, defined by the cut and the cloth. And—I'm only a little ashamed to say—by the labels. This morning I'm wearing black leather lace-up shoes by Santoni, Gene Meyer socks, Hanro boxers, a white cotton shirt by Missoni, and a charcoal gray two-piece suit by Loro Piana. There's a Gianfranco Ferre belt around my waist and a white linen Claytons handkerchief in my top pocket. I don't wear a tie—I'm only going to school, after all.

Okay, so this outfit is a bit over the top, even for me. But I feel like treating myself. I still feel a bit uncomfortable about what happened with Eddie last night. I can't believe he attacked me like that. And I didn't try to protect myself, I just ran. What does that say about me? Well, let's not go there.

Why did I say those things last night? Why couldn't I have just lied and said that I lusted after Joanna Stevens like everyone else? Would that have been so difficult? Even saying nothing would have been better than admitting to finding Helen attractive. And that's all I *had* said really. Why had Eddie twisted it? I don't know.

But I'm a different person this morning. In Eddie's eyes at least, I'm a pervert and a coward. I'm avoiding asking myself if that's how I now see myself too. A coward, I mean. I know that I'm not a pervert. Wonder if Eddie will spread it all around the class?

I saunter into the kitchen. It's huge and perfect, as you'd expect, all chrome and bleached wood and Italian tiles on the floor. It's all Mom's doing; God, but she does have exquisite taste. It's where Madeleine gets it from, for sure. But it's icy in the kitchen, even though Mom is there, a picture of Gucci and Prada casuals. It's too perfect, the kitchen, if you know what I mean. Not even a crumb lying around, not the least indication that any cooking has ever been done in there.

"Hi Mom."

She looks up from where she's sitting at a counter, ingesting rye-toast—as if by osmosis, the feeble nibbles she's taking. She's not wearing sunglasses for once and she looks at me as I look back at her.

"God, Tom, what's happened to your face?"

She's genuinely concerned, so the redness and the swelling must be obvious after all, and I've been deluding myself that no one will notice it. Sometimes we all do that, don't we? See things the way we'd like them to be, I mean, rather than seeing them the way they actually, obviously, are.

"It's nothing, really. Just an accident."

This is not a conversation I want to have. In part, I've dressed to provoke her. I want her to tell me that I am overdressed for school. She has a way of saying it so that I can tell that she thinks I'm looking sharp. I like the buzz that that gives me, her appreciation of how I look and what I'm wearing. I'm going to be disappointed this morning and I might as well be honest with you; I don't take disappointment well. I mean, I don't throw tantrums or anything, but it gets bottled up inside me and it can be days before I'm feeling loose and normal again.

"How did it happen?"

She's up off her seat now and I can't turn around and walk out. She comes towards me with a look of motherly concern on her beautifully made-up face. A hand reaches up as though gently to touch the swelling, but I turn away. The hand goes down but she is still there as I turn back to face her. I notice a slight crumb at the corner of her mouth and I absently brush it away, like I'm the parent somehow and she is the child.

I can smell her perfume from here; Enigma, by Alexandra de Markoff, all rose and iris and jasmine.

"Leave it Mom, it's nothing."

I turn away again and she knows I'm hiding something. She's not stupid, after all.

"You haven't been fighting, have you?"

Her tone suggests that she can't imagine I'm capable of fighting. I don't know how I feel about that; I mean, it's true to say that

I've never been *involved* in a fight, but I've never considered myself to be soft. And the fact that I dress the way I do and haven't been bullied would suggest that there isn't a *general perception* that I'm feeble. At least, I think that's how it works. Of course, there's the question of last night and the business with Eddie, but like I said, I am in no mood to pursue that train of thought.

"You're not being bullied are you darling?"

It's like she's reading my mind. In a way, I wish she was. Evidently she finds the thought of me fighting unlikely and she's taken the next logical step and assumed that I must be a helpless victim or something. And what cuts like a cold blade is the fact that nothing in her tone suggests that she finds *this* unbelievable. So in her eyes there's no chance I could be a fighter, but a feeble loser victim is something she *can* see in me.

I'm not getting what I want here so I might as well get out, go to school. It's sunny and it won't hurt to hang out at the bus stop and take in some rays. I'm going to need my books and some shades—Fendi black wrap-arounds with this suit, I think—and they are back up in my room.

"Tom, if you want to stay home from school and talk…"

I hear her calling after me as I stomp up the stairs but I ignore her. I grab the briefcase with my books in it and slide on the shades. In moments I'm out on the landing again, heading for the stairs.

"Tom… come in here a minute."

Madeleine's door is ajar. I push it open and step inside. Madeleine is dressed—blue Versace skinny jeans and a white cotton Fiorucci top—and sits at her dressing table brushing her hair. She turns and looks at me. Just the briefest part of a second and just the briefest movement of her eyes and I know that she is giving me the once over.

"Looking very very sharp, Tom. Too cool for school."

Right now I want to kiss her for that. I want to hold her and I want her to hold me and I want to kiss her. But of course, I don't. I stand here, gently nodding my agreement, because I *do* look sharp.

"Looking good yourself, sis."

Trust Madeleine to know exactly what I want and to give it to me. I just love her to bits. I think I might have said that before.

CHAPTER 3

Who's that girl?

There's no one about at the bus stop. It's too early for kids going to school and trust me, no one from this part of town travels to *work* by bus. Just look at the road. Already it's like a Mercedes and BMW convention.

No sign of the bus, so you'd think I'd sit down on the little wooden bench right there next to the bus stop. But look at it; peeling paint and the wood beginning to splinter. And I'm wearing a Loro Piana suit, remember? I set my briefcase down on the bench though, and open it. I reach in and take a slim, worn, paperback volume out. It's a pocket edition of a book that is dear to me. It's a book I like to carry with me most of the time. Nearly all of the time, if I'm honest; and I *am* trying to be honest talking to you.

I don't need to scan the cover, and I slip it neatly into an inside pocket. It's a pocket edition, I told you. I feel comfortable with it sitting there, out of sight but next to my heart.

Anyway, the bus is here and I'd better move it. At least it will be too early for Eddie; I can delay that pleasure, and that's a relief. I can watch the houses and the fields and the cars as the bus passes them by. It's an uneventful journey.

I get to school and there's no one around. Well, some of the teachers are here I suppose; cars are already parked in the lot. The doors will be open too and there will be somebody in the library, so that's where I'll go, even though it's sunny out and all. Don't think that I'm some kind of super-nerd or something; this is not something I'd normally do. But today, I don't want to be standing outside when people arrive.

I particularly don't want to be cutting a lonely figure when Eddie arrives.

So I go to the library, and you know what? When I'm in there, damned if I can settle and read anything, damned if I can. Does that ever happen to you? You have this big idea that you are going to read this or that, and it's hours away and you tell yourself yeah, it'll be just great to read this or that and you work yourself into a state of anticipation and then when the time comes, you just somehow don't feel like making the effort? Well maybe it's just me. Sometimes I wonder if I'm crazy. I really do.

Turning the pages of the book in front of me, I'm not reading any of the words. I'm not even really looking at the pictures, and they're wonderful photographs of the treasures from the tomb of Tutankhamen, the Egyptian boy-king who died a goddamn million years ago. Well, a few thousand years ago, so it might as well have been a million; it's not like there's a chance I could have known him or anything. Anyway, I'm just turning pages and not really reading or looking, so what does it matter?

It's an hour later and I'm out in the yard. There's lots of kids around now and there's yelling and games going on, and laughing and stuff. And it somehow feels safe though God knows why it should. It's not as if all these kids—who don't know me or owe me anything—will suddenly become my shield if Eddie shows up and decides he wants to trample me into the dust.

I'm looking around—trying to spot Eddie, of course—and I can't see him. But getting back to that point, it's interesting isn't it, the idea that there's safety in numbers? Here in the school yard, that's just crap and you know it as well as I do. If you're getting beaten into chopped meat, all a crowd of school kids will do is gather round to get the best view. You've done it. We all have. What the numbers do, I guess, is act like a shield you can *hide* behind while your eyes are constantly scanning for danger. It gives you a chance to see before you're seen, if you know what I mean.

Except that *I* stand out don't I? I can't hide in this crowd. Dressed the way I am, it's like I have a neon arrow pointing at me. And what makes me stand out even more is the nature of this school.

You will have got the picture, I'm thinking, that dear old Mom and Dad can afford the finest private education that money can buy. Well let me tell you, there's nothing private-sector or privileged about the environment that they've put me into. I asked them once why I didn't go to some snotty private academic factory.

"We don't believe that wealth should be used to buy a head start in life, dear.'

That's Mom. Isn't it enough to make you puke?

"It's a question of social justice."

Dad now, at his most preachy and sanctimonious so that it's all you can do not to fall asleep where you stand.

"Everyone should have an equal start in life and achievement should be based on merit."

How I don't fall over and beat my fists against the carpet with laughter when he comes out with this crap is beyond me. I'm mentally strong—that must be it.

"And if it was good enough for Paul McCartney's children..."

Mom again. I have to put my hand over my mouth in case I do *indeed* have to hold back the vomit. Tell me, have you ever heard such ill-conceived drivel? It's not like Mom is stupid or anything. She's really smart and well-read. And she's a partner in some hot-shot PR agency for the sake of the Lord! And yet somehow she's convinced herself that it's perfectly reasonable to base the way she chooses to educate her children on something she's read about some geriatric pop star! I imagine that you, not knowing her, must think that she is on drugs or something. It gets worse though. Dad's a lawyer. You'd think that *that* would make him pragmatic or something. You'd think that wouldn't you? And he must be, in so many other regards, because he is incredibly successful. Incredibly. Really, he is.

I did wonder, once, whether they were perhaps too stingy to spend money on a private education, but they are not stingy people, either of them. Look at the clothes allowance that Madeleine and I enjoy. No, not stingy. Not stingy at all. So I guess it's all down to some kind of hippy idealism. Goddamn morons.

The other thing is, I think that having gone to all the trouble of having us and all, to complete the checklist and all that, they perhaps wanted us to be around, to be on show when people came around, like the Mercedes and the BMW. So we have to go to a local school. And *that* thought does make you want to puke, doesn't it? Sure it does.

Actually, I have no problem with the school. I mean, it's nothing special and the teachers do their best, I guess. Even if in some cases, like McGregor who teaches physics, that isn't saying much. On the whole, it could be much worse.

Oh shit. There's Eddie... And the point I was trying to make about me in this school? Well let's just say that this is a crowd that I can't hide in. I mean, take a look around. How many other kids do you see wearing a Loro Piana suit? I must stand out like a whore in a church.

Despite the glowing radioactive nature of my appearance, Eddie hasn't noticed me. It's not encouraging to see him with Dougan and Fletcher though. Look at them all coming through the gates, hoodies up and swaggering. They walk with that affected swing of the shoulders like they're straight out of South Central LA or something. I particularly like the way that Dougan smokes with the cigarette just hanging out of his mouth. If you see him up close while he's doing it, you realize that he hasn't got the hang of it; the smoke drifts into his eyes and he constantly has to squint like some inbred retard. That kills me. It really does. Not that I laugh in his face. He doesn't have a sense of humor, Dougan. And Eddie is a different person when he's with these two. I wonder if Eddie has said anything about last night to them. What am I saying? Of course he has. How could he not? You would, wouldn't you? And yeah, so would I.

I'm making myself as inconspicuous as I can in the hope that they don't notice me. There's only a minute or two before the bell goes and there will be at least the temporary sanctuary of the classroom. I'm looking around and oh—it's her. Sitting on the dry grass shaded by the tree, she's reading a book. Who? Oh right, that girl I was telling Eddie about last night—not Helen, not his sister; the other one, remember? No, that's right, I *didn't* tell him, did I? I kept her to myself. Well she's sitting right there under a tree reading a book. She's not more than a few yards away. She's got this thick, wavy black hair that falls over her shoulders. It's very dark without quite being black really. It's as near to black as hair gets without using some coloring agent. Her hair has not really been cut or styled or shaped, but it's very attractive all the same. Her skin is quite pale in contrast, like it doesn't get exposed to the sun much. I like that. There's nothing worse than these orange-skinned girls you see. Do they really think that we're fooled into believing they've been to Barbados or Tahiti or something? Joanna Stevens has skin like that. It's less Acapulco and more the local tanning salon and it shows. You just don't see girls in Acapulco with orange skin. These orange girls, like Joanna Stevens, they just make me want to puke. They really do.

But this girl under the tree is pale. And she's sitting with her legs crossed under her and her shoes kicked off and all, and she's wearing this sort of burgundy dress that's very fine corduroy. It's not particularly fashionable and I'm guessing it's not particularly new either, because there is a slight fade to the color and some very slight fraying of the corduroy at the edges. I've noticed her wearing it before and I guess I like to see her in it. It's kind of bohemian and hippy, and you'd think I'd be snobbish about that, me being obsessed with fashion and all, but it's the girl *wearing* the dress who *makes* the dress is what I think. At least it's what I think in this girl's case.

I realize that I'm kind of staring at her. I'm not worried about that though; she'll never notice me—she's too wrapped up in that book. She's looking at the pages very intense, like she's trying to suck the words up from the paper through her narrow black-framed glasses and directly into her brain. I'm getting a kick out of watching her read in that way. I always get a kick out of watching someone reading when they're really concentrating on something. It's like what they're doing is the only thing in the universe, and even though everything is going on around them they are never aware of it; it's like they've found a *new* universe in the words on the page and they're hell bent on living there and not here. It would be a neat trick if you could pull it off. Anywhere would be better than here.

Another thing I'm noticing about her is the white cotton blouse she's wearing. It's long-sleeved and sits under the dress and you can see that it's not expensive or anything, but the sleeves flare slightly at the cuffs and there's some ever so slightly pink embroidery at the edges. It's so cute it all but stops your heart. I swear that it does.

And do you know something? I've been so wrapped up in watching this girl that I've forgotten about Eddie.

"Hey pervert!"

It's a loud shout even though Eddie is quite obviously standing right behind me. It's funny, but right away I'm aware that everyone in the yard has stopped what they're doing and they're turning to watch. Kids can sniff out humiliation like a dog sniffs out crap. And if you ever get the chance to watch, look at their faces: glee. They're relishing what they're about to see. Kids are bastards. They really are.

Well I don't get the opportunity to respond to Eddie; I don't know what I'd say anyway. Probably something witty for sure. Something to turn Perez Hilton green. But like I say, I don't get the chance because next thing I know I'm shoved in the back, and as I stumble forward a leg sticks out to trip me. Catches me on the shin actually and hurts like a bastard right away. But it sends my briefcase flying and I go crashing into the tree where the girl is sitting so that she has to roll to get out of the way when I fall. I fall exactly where she was sitting and my face feels like it's exploding with pain because I've hit the tree with my face, right where Eddie caught me last night with his fist. It's throbbing so bad that I'd like to cry out or whimper or something, but I don't. I'm lying on my back wondering if my suit is ruined and thinking that the best I can hope for is that it's creased and I'll have to suffer it not hanging well for a day.

I'm lying on my back, squinting up at the sky through the branches of the tree and through the faces peering down at me like I'm a carnival freak that they've paid to see. You should watch the faces of people when they're looking at freaks—it would have to be on TV now of course—but you'll see that there is a fascination. People don't know it, but there is the hint of a smile on their faces as they stare at something unfortunate. People are bastards. They really are. When you laugh at someone who has an accident, like in those crappy TV shows where they suck idiots into sending in home videos— have these people *no* shame?—it's called *schadenfreude*. Trust the Germans to have a word for it. But that's kind of okay really, because it's just an accident, and it could happen to anyone now and then, who doesn't think things through. What I'm talking about is looking at unfortunate people who can't help being the way they are. Most people don't laugh out loud at *them*. But if you look at someone's face when they are watching people who are not ordinary like themselves, then you'll see what I'm talking about. It's not nice. It really isn't.

And that's what I see in the faces looking down at me now. I'm squinting of course because my sunglasses have gone flying. But I can still see Eddie snarling down at me from inside the dark hood he's wearing, and the faces of the gleeful crowd. Bastards. But it's Eddie's face I'm fixed on.

"Steer clear of my sister, pervert."

Lying there, I can almost hear the thoughts of the crowd as they wonder just what might have gone on between Eddie's kid sister and me. She goes to *this* school, so it occurs to me, the way it obviously hasn't occurred to Eddie, that Helen's life is not going to be easy in the next few days. The speculation will become ever more salacious too, because we're talking about kids here. And I've already mentioned what kids are. I'm one myself really, so I do know what I'm talking about.

I don't respond to Eddie. I just lie there, on my back. I don't even try to get up. Eddie is staring right down at me and his face is contorted with rage. I just take deep breaths.

Then I'm saved by the bell. It's obvious that there is not going to be any more action—largely because I'm not going to react, and partly because Eddie doesn't seem inclined to just kick me to death—so the crowd disperses and heads in a shapeless mass for the school doors. And—

I'm not making this up—you can actually *feel* their collective disappointment. Really, you can.

Eddie is one of the last to leave and can't help himself, but he has to scowl a last few words.

"Pay attention to what I've told you, pervert."

I do wish he'd stop calling me that. And then you know what he does? Can you believe this? He spits on the ground next to my head—I don't know if that was a bad aim or a good one really. Yes, he spits. I'm guessing that Eddie is no longer my best friend.

So I take a few breaths and when I think everyone is gone, I roll over and get to my knees, and I knock the dust off my sleeves and begin to straighten myself out. And actually I'm not alone at all, because *she's* standing there.

I know she's there because I can see her bare feet and the hem of that burgundy corduroy dress, so I look up. The sun is behind her and it seems to make her hair glow red and warm at the edges, like you see in fancy magazine ads. They've gone out of their way to achieve the effect in those photographs and you know that it's phony when you look at them. But this is just a happy circumstance and you know, I think that it's truly beautiful. I really do.

"Are you okay?"

"Yeah, sure. Thanks."

She's holding my sunglasses in one hand. Holding them out for me to take, so I take them and blow the dust off them and slip them on. It makes me feel a little bit better just doing that. In her other hand she's holding a book and I recognise it. It's my book. I pat my pocket just to be sure, but I'm sure all right, and my book must have gone flying when I hit the tree. She holds the book out to me, looking down at the cover. I can see the pink embroidery on the cuff of her sleeve and it really is delicate. Truly lovely.

"*The Catcher in the Rye*... do you like this?"

She has a pleasant voice. It's soft and it's not challenging at all. You know how with most girls, everything is a challenge? Everything is a test? Well *her* voice, it just doesn't give me that impression. I might be wrong and she might be just too damned clever at disguising her intentions and all, but it doesn't feel like that.

"I'm carrying it around, so you'd *think* that I like it, wouldn't you?"

That doesn't come out the way I want it to and with her being nice to me and all, it just makes me seem like a jerk. I take the book from her hand and slip it back into my pocket without looking at the cover.

"I'm sorry. Sure I like it. It's a particular favorite if you really want to know."

She smiles like she was never offended in the first place. But you can never tell with girls. I can never tell what the hell they're thinking most of the time. I wish to God I could, I really do.

"I'd tell you all about it but the bell's rang. We don't want to be late."

I'm standing as I speak, and I don't think that my suit has suffered much. I'm dusting it off and straightening it out, watching her as she picks up her own book and the bookmarker she is using. She's lost her page but she doesn't seem to mind; she just tosses that book into her straw bag as she slips into her flat black shoes. The shoes are scuffed slightly—not much, but enough for me to notice, yet they look very comfortable. I can see her toes wiggling in them.

I wander over to where my briefcase has fallen and I pick it up as I turn to her.

"I guess we'd better hurry."

She's heard me but she doesn't answer right away. She looks over at the school doors. The last few dawdlers are drifting inside.

"I don't really want to today."

She looks up at the sky and stretches as she speaks. The white cotton of her blouse is brilliant in the sunshine and she is so close that I can smell her. She smells of soap—clean and fresh and fragrant and it's all I can do to keep from burying my nose in her thick hair, just to take in that beautiful scent. Have you noticed that, the way that girls always have amazing smelling hair? Well it's true, they do. It's a fact, I swear it. And it's definitely something to do with being a girl because God knows, every guy I know uses the same shampoos and conditioners and stuff that girls use, but how often do you find yourself wanting to bury your nose in a guy's hair, eh? Answer me that. I mean, I don't know from experience, but I don't imagine even gay guys go around burying their noses in other guys' hair. It's unheard of. But when those shampoos and conditioners come together with girls, the combination is wonderful and intoxicating. You want to know what I think? I think that old Mother Nature can see into the future, and for a long time now she's been genetically preparing girls so that they'll be able to react in a special way with the shampoos and conditioners and all the other hair-care stuff and soaps and moisturizers that are available now. I know how that sounds and I'm prepared to have you think I'm crazy, but tell me if you have a better explanation. Do you? Thought not. And what it's done, then, this trick of Mother Nature's, is it's turned girls into wild flowers in a way. They become fragrant and sweet.

This girl is Mother Nature's orchid.

"You want to do something different today?"

Have I really heard her say that?

"What, cut school altogether?"

Way to sound like a retard, right? But she's kind and indulgent.

"Yeah, sure. Come on—what's one day?"

Before I know what I've done we're out through the school gates and she's walking faster and is a little way ahead. Just who is this girl?

CHAPTER 4

Carve his name with pride

We've turned left out of the school gate. She's walking a few steps ahead of me and she doesn't look back. Clearly, this day away from school is something she was going to enjoy anyway, with or without me. Not that I was thinking that it had been a spontaneous suggestion on her part, with her seeing my humiliation as an opportunity to spend some time alone with me or anything. I'm not that vain. Hell, who am I kidding? Of course I'm that vain. And actually I am somewhat deflated to realize that I've not become the center of her universe. See what I mean about girls? I don't have a clue what the hell goes on in their minds. I swear I don't.

So anyway, I increase my stride and in a few steps I'm right there next to her. We walk down the street, past the row of ratty looking stores. I can't help gazing at these storefronts with their peeling paint and cracked windows and general air of decay. There are five of them together in a two-story block. I guess that when they were built, the idea was that the owners would literally live above the store. Maybe they still do, but you wouldn't really want to. Many of the windows that I can see on the upper floor are broken, and filthy gray *voile* nets hang behind them. As I try to imagine people living in the rooms beyond, just one word comes to mind: squalor.

I try to picture these stores as they would have been when they were first built; clean, with sparkling windows and filled with new stock and optimistic storekeepers and their families, all looking forward to a bright tomorrow. Thing is, I just can't get that feeling. I usually can. Usually I have a great imagination, but this is asking too much of it.

Carve his name with pride

The neighborhood that these stores were built to serve, well, we're walking past what's left of it right now. This whole area is a demolition site. Most of the houses were condemned a long time ago and just a few ragged and lonely looking brick structures remain. You can't believe that people still live in these places, but they do. Poor, rootless souls that everyone has forgotten about. The sense of dereliction is overwhelming and depressing. I'm depressed just walking through it. And it's been like this for years now. Dead, empty land, strewn with demolition rubble. It's owned by some big-shot property developers and they're obviously in no rush to go ahead and actually develop. And in the meantime the city has to live with this rotting cancer right in its heart. I wonder where the property developers live. Right next door to me, probably. Property developers can be bastards.

In all this time, while I've been thinking, we've been walking, side by side. The sun has unfurled his wings and the day is definitely becoming hot. Funny how I think of the sun as being male. I think of the moon as being female. And come to think of it, I'm not alone in

53

this. In French the sun is *le soleil*—a masculine word. The moon is *la lune*—a feminine word. It cracks me up how some languages divide inanimate objects by gender. I mean, can't you just picture it? A suave masculine French mirror coming on to a saucy feminine table? You can't? Well it cracks *me* up at any rate. And in German, some words are neuter. *Neuter*, for God's sake! Books are neuter in German. Poor old books—the eunuchs of the German-speaking world.

Anyway, this is what I'm thinking as I walk along with this girl. I'm probably thinking all this babble because we haven't exchanged so much as a single word yet and to tell the truth, I don't know what to say. I'm not nervous around girls as a rule, even if I don't have a clue what they want or what they're thinking. I don't think it's her though; I think it's because I'm conscious of walking through a demolition site wearing a sharp suit and carrying a briefcase. This is not an environment I'm entirely comfortable with.

"Where are we going?"

I have to ask, if only to break the silence that I'm now conscious of and which is starting to bug me a little.

The girl stops and turns to me, smiling so that I can see the edges of her straight, white teeth.

"I win."

Then she giggles and brings up a hand to cover her mouth. I never saw anything so cute in all my life, I swear to God.

"Just a game I was playing. Wondering who would say something first."

See what I mean about girls? How can you possibly know what's going on with them? I mean, I've spent tons of time with my sister and we're really close and everything, but I still haven't got a clue what's going on with her most of the time. It's exasperating. It really is. But the thing about girls is, despite everything, despite not having a clue about them or anything, they're just lovely. Girls are just lovely and you love being around them. Isn't that how it is? It is with me, at any rate.

"Well I'm happy that you've won."

I'm trying to act all adult now, like I'm above her childish game, though truth is, I'm finding it all cute as hell.

"Now can you just tell me where we're going?"

She turns and begins to walk on, and in a stride I'm beside her again.

"Don't you just like to walk?"

Now what can I say to a question like that? Of course I don't just like to walk. Does anybody? But it's obvious that she wants me to think that *she* might just like to walk. Could be that she's trying to trick me. She likes playing games. Girls. Christ!

"No. Not really." I decide that honesty is the best policy for now. "So where *are* we going?"

"It doesn't matter. Just walking. Come on, it'll do you good."

And then she does the damndest thing. We're wandering along, side by side in the sunshine, among the ruins, and I feel her hand just slide into mine. Just like that, without looking, in one smooth movement like it's the most natural thing in the world. And don't get me wrong here, it's not as though I don't like it. I can feel the soft embroidered cuff of her blouse pressed gently against my wrist and it's so lovely that I have to concentrate in order to just breathe properly. Her hand is very soft and smooth. And very warm. And dry. I hate it when you hold hands with a girl and it's all hot and wet and sweaty. All the time you want to let go and wash your hand but you know you can't because it would be a cruel thing to do and she doesn't deserve to be hurt or humiliated or anything. But all you can do is fight back a grimace and wait until you can rush off to where there is soap and water and clean towels. Well *her* hand is not like that at all. If you want to know, it's lovely. It really is.

So we're walking for a while and not saying much, and we've left the dereliction far behind. We're off the road altogether and we're in this amazing place. I don't know it—I've never been here before—but we're walking along a path that winds through deciduous woodland with the huge trees shading us from the fierce heat of the sun. The land is not flat and in the hollows there are a couple of fair-sized lakes and the trees go right down to the edge of the water. And there's a small brook. We can hear it but not see it yet.

There isn't even the hint of a breeze and while we walk along the shingle path, I catch the scent of her hair. I can't help myself. I lean just a little closer, so that my nose is almost touching her hair and I breathe in deeply.

That stops her. She turns to me.

"What was that all about?"

She's not angry or upset or scared or anything. Well, she doesn't seem to be. But it's obviously a new experience for her. What can I say?

"It's just your hair. It smells really... lovely."

She lets go of my hand and although she does it in a gentle way so that I know that it's not a gesture of rejection, I'm momentarily depressed. That surprises me. I'm usually pretty cool about things like that. But she never takes her eyes off mine as she reaches up and takes hold of her hair, pulling it from behind her smooth, pale neck, and she's sort of offering it to me. I close my eyes and lean forward until my nose is buried in those soft black waves. I don't think there's been a more beautiful moment in history. There hasn't been, I swear to God.

And after a moment she lets her hair fall, and it glides back into place, cascading about her shoulders. Then she takes my hand again and we're walking, towards the sound of the brook.

Before you know it, we're in this sort of clearing, and we're sitting right by the edge of the brook, shaded by a big willow tree that must be a million years old at least. Thing is,

I don't mind sitting on the grass here, even though I am wearing a suit. It's very dry. The brook is slow and lazy next to where we're sitting, but we can hear it gently babbling downstream. It must narrow and run shallow over rocks and pebbles down there. If you must know, it's very lovely. It really is.

"It's lovely here. It really is."

She looks over at me from where she's sitting, kinda sideways, and there is this glint in her eyes so that I wonder what she's going to say.

"Yes, it is. It really is."

I *could* wonder if she's mocking me or something. But like I've said, you just can't understand girls. Then she laughs and kicks off her shoes and turns so that her feet can dangle in the brook. She leans back on her hands and turns her face to the sky with her eyes closed. I've never seen contentment like it, I swear to God, and if I could just bottle this moment and sell it I'd be a billionaire in no time.

I'm looking down at the lazy flow of the water, watching the sparkle of the sunlight on the surface and her toes wiggling below.

"You should try this. Come on, kick your shoes off."

"And ruin a pair of Gene Meyer socks?"

To me that's a joke, but she doesn't laugh. Instead she's looking at me like she's all of a sudden wondering why she's brought me here.

"You sit there dressed like that and you look for all the world like a lawyer. This isn't a place for lawyers."

Well what do you say to that, exactly? I'm wondering whether it's a sign she wants me to leave. Well I don't know what I'm doing here in the first place, so maybe I should.

"My dad's a lawyer."

Could I possibly have said anything lamer?

"You *don't* say. But *you're not* one, right? Not yet at any rate. So chill out and enjoy the day."

"I am enjoying it."

"Are you?"

"Yes, I'm enjoying the goddamn day. I really am. And I have no intention whatsoever of becoming a goddamn lawyer."

And that's true; I've been to Dad's office a few times. It's like goddamn death row in there, and even the secretaries, who mostly are beautiful, daren't smile. And you can see that they'd be really happy and cheerful if it was allowed, and that they're repressing their true natures. I shouldn't wonder if they become wild drunken licentious sluts on the weekends. Now that *would* be something to see. I don't get into the city much at night though.

She just nods a little and purses her lips.

"Is that right, Holden? You've no intention of becoming a goddamn lawyer?"

Now right away I know that there's something going on here. I know exactly what she means when she calls me *Holden*, and I'm sure you've figured it out too. Holden Caulfield is the narrator of the goddamn book I carry around with me, *The Catcher in the Rye*.

"Why did you just call me Holden?"

"Isn't he your hero? Don't you model yourself on him?"

"I haven't a clue what you're talking about."

"Well, you carry a copy of *The Catcher in the Rye* around with you."

"Have you read it?

"More than once. But not as often as you I'll bet. I don't carry it next to my heart."

"So I like it. So what? I still don't see why you'd call *me* Holden."

"Because you talk like old Holden. I thought you were doing it on goddamn purpose. I really did."

Oh that was cute. She's very sharp, this girl, I'm realizing that. And clever. And it looks like she's well read. I kinda like clever girls, especially if they're well read. I can't stand it when you go out with a girl, and you've taken time with the way you look, and you've taken trouble in thinking about where to take her, and all the time you are with her, all she can talk about is some goddamn celebrity or other. You try to discuss philosophy or current affairs, say, but all she can talk about, because it's all she knows, is what happened to the latest celebrity retard. *Celebretards* is what Madeleine calls them, these moronic products of vacuous reality TV shows. I think Madeleine invented the word. She might have done. Madeleine is very clever. Anyway, a lot of girls *are* like that. A lot of boys too, but I don't care about *them*. I don't want to be dating any goddamn boys.

"I don't talk like Holden Caulfield."

I can't look her in the eye as I say it, because while it's never really occurred to me before, I realize that there's some truth in what she's saying, maybe.

She laughs out loud.

"Oh come on. Tell me you do it on purpose—you must do."

"Actually, no. I mean, I'll take your goddamn word for it. But no, I don't do it on purpose. *Really I don't.*"

This time she sees that I'm making a joke of it all and she smiles.

"You don't mind if *I* call you Holden though?"

"Well, the thing is, yes I do. I'm happy with my own name. And in any case, I'm in no way as cynical as Holden Caulfield."

And I think that's the truth. Holden Caulfield is a cynical, complex and contradictory person, wouldn't you say? I'm really quite simple and straightforward. I don't think I'm like him at all. Really, I'm not.

"I'm going to call you Holden anyway. I think it suits you."

She swings her feet out of the brook and rests them on the tinder-dry grass. Water droplets trickle down her ankles and sink into the ground. I take the Claytons linen handkerchief from my pocket and offer it to her.

"What's that for?"

"To dry your feet with. I don't imagine you're carrying a towel around with you in that bag.'

She seems genuinely astonished.

"You're quite a gentleman, Holden. Thanks."

I watch her as she carefully dries the water from her toes with my handkerchief.

"You know something. While we're on the subject of names, I don't actually know yours."

She stops dabbing at her toes for a moment and looks up.

"Really? But we've been going to the same school for years."

"I've seen you around from time to time, but that's all."

I don't know whether or not she's hurt by this. It's hard to tell. I don't feel comfortable enough to tell her that I've liked her for a long time and kept it all to myself.

"Sylvia. You can call me whatever you like."

The mood has definitely grown a tad heavier.

"Sylvia is good. It's lovely."

And if you want to know, I truly think that it is. It has the ring of tiny glass bells to it when you say it. They're barely audible drifting on a background breeze. That's how it feels to me.

"No wonder you feel happy here. This is your environment isn't it?"

"What do you mean?"

She's handing back my handkerchief but she's looking directly into my eyes. Her question isn't a challenge; it's a genuine request for knowledge.

I squeeze the handkerchief gently in my hand for a moment, feeling it damp and soft, and for some crazy reason valuing it more because it has touched her feet.

"Well we're here, in this woodland, and Sylvia comes from the Latin word *silva*, which means woodland. That's what I meant."

Now she smiles.

"Yes it does. I bet there's only you and me at that whole goddamn school who would know that, wouldn't you say?"

I'm not going to rise to that.

"Maybe. But listen, just in case you ever feel like using it, my name's…"

"Tom. Yes I know."

I must look surprised. I *am* surprised.

"Oh, come on. Look at yourself. Everybody knows Tom Hathaway. It's not like you go out of your way to blend in, is it?"

I have to admit this. To myself, if not to her. I must say, though, that I truly had no idea that I was some kind of school *celebretard*.

"I'm still going to call you Holden though."

"Whatever."

I'm getting used to the idea now. And what I like is that I'm getting the feeling that Sylvia and I are going to see more of each other, and I'm really going to like that.

We're walking through the trees now

and it's late in the afternoon. She's tucked her shoes into her bag and she's walking barefoot.

"Do you hate the movies as much as Holden Caulfield hates them?"

"No."

And it's true, I don't. I quite like them actually. Not all of them of course.

"So would you like to go with me sometime?"

Would I?

"Sure. That sounds nice."

She seems genuinely pleased and that pleases me.

"Would you like my telephone number? You could call me..."

She's sounding a little hesitant now, as though she's put herself out on the line and she's not sure what my response will be. It's kind of touching, actually, since this is the first time in the whole day that I haven't felt that she's one step ahead of me.

I take the phone from my pocket and offer it to her.

"Here, put your number in this."

She reaches out to take it with her left hand and that cute embroidered cuff rides up a tad and I can't help but stare. She notices and pulls her hand back but it's too late because I've seen. On the inside of her wrist and extending up her arm farther than I can see there are scars. Some of them look old and some of them look newer. But they are all from deep cuts and that is for certain. I've never seen anything like it, I swear to God.

She's turned away from me and I'm standing, holding out the phone. What can I say? Should I say anything? I don't want to talk to the back of her head. And do you know what? I think she's started to cry. I really do. And it damn near breaks your heart, doesn't it, to see a girl like that crying?

"Hey, don't cry."

She's not sobbing or anything, but there are tears rolling from her eyes as she turns to me.

"Let's just go home and forget that today ever happened."

That's not what I want.

"There's no need for that. And anyway, I thought we were going to the movies sometime."

Even I'm smart enough to realize that it's the wrong time to ask about those scars.

The tears are still trickling down her face and I am glad for her sake that she is not wearing make-up, because she'd be looking like Alice Cooper right about now if she was.

"You'd still want to go? Even now?"

"Sure I would. Why wouldn't I?"

She's pretty vulnerable now, not the confident happy girl who led me into this place earlier. I want to hold her, but I daren't, not just yet.

"You've seen. And you still want to go to see a movie with me?"

"Of course I do. Nothing's changed."

And it hasn't. I really *do* want to go out with her, no matter what.

"Then I want you to see."

She begins to unbutton that cute little embroidered cuff.

"There's no need…"

"No, really, I want you to see. I don't want you to think that I've got anything to hide."

Still the tears are running down her pale cheeks as she rolls up her sleeve. I reach out with my handkerchief, still a little damp from drying her feet, and gently wipe them away. The goddamn handkerchief will take on the aura of a holy relic before the day is through at this rate.

God but it's a terrible sight to see. It really is. There are criss-crossing scars all the way up to the inside of her elbow. And some of the scars are like letters and they spell out a word that you can read as plain as anything. And I swear to God that the word that they spell out is *Tom*.

CHAPTER 5

What moms can be

Mom's car is sitting in the driveway, so she's home. I've been in a great mood right up to this very moment, what with spending the day with Sylvia and all. Now I'm nervous seeing Mom's car. She's never normally home at this time and I wonder if it's anything to do with me.

All kinds of thoughts race through my mind and I bet you know how that is for yourself. Has the school called *her* to ask where I am? Has she got it into her head that I'm being bullied at school and called *them*? You know the kind of crap I mean. Fact is, it's probably nothing to do with me at all, but I can really be self-centered like that.

The worst thing about this, as I fumble in my pocket to retrieve my door key, is that it's steered my thoughts away from Sylvia. All the way home I've been thinking about Sylvia and now the goddamn BMW 525 sits midnight blue and polished in the driveway and Sylvia just dissolves away. Just like that.

My key slides into the lock and the door opens and I'm in. I think about trying to sneak upstairs to my room. I want to change out of this suit and into something more casual to lounge in while I mull over the day with Sylvia again.

But I don't sneak up the stairs. I'm standing in the hallway holding my briefcase when Mom steps out of the kitchen. She has the goddamn phone glued to her ear. She's not speaking but she's sure as hell listening and she's not going to break off to speak to me. She's not going to let me sneak off either though; she's beckoning me into the kitchen. At least she doesn't seem upset about anything, but who can tell?

So I follow her through into the sterile capsule of marble, tiles and polished chrome and I plonk myself on a stool at the breakfast bar, waiting while she finishes her call. I'm watching her as she wanders slowly around the kitchen. Her feet almost slide across the tiles and every now and then she does this sort of pirouette, where she lifts herself up on her toes and spins around, still talking and listening. It's as cute as hell, really, but right now I don't find anything to smile about as I sit and await her pleasure.

I hate the way that people live for their phones. It's as if they simply have to be in constant and instant communication with everyone they know. They're talking or texting just about constantly. It's a wonder that anything ever gets done. And okay, I have a phone myself, as you know, and I carry it with me, as you are aware. Not that I get a lot of calls, and I rarely make them. And I sure as hell haven't got caught up in the text mania. I haven't sent a goddamn text in my life and I never will, I swear to God. I hate it, just walking down the street and seeing just about everyone with a phone glued to their ear, or walking in a slow-motion daze composing inane text messages to send to their vacuous friends. Kids are the worst, I admit it. If you added it up, I'd hate to think how many hours of each day kids waste sending stupid messages. But it's not *just* kids.

*Hello? Hello? It's me... I SAID IT'S ME... I'm on the train / bus / tram / ferry—*substitute whatever you like, but I'll bet that that's a conversation you've heard more than once. And just what the hell is the point of a conversation like that? For the sake of the Lord, can't you imagine that the person at the other end couldn't have worked it out in most cases?

And you'd have to say that America became a superpower without everyone wearing their thumbs out banging out texts to each other about the color of shoes or something stupid. And you know, England built an empire that spanned the world when there were just sailing ships and written letters. I guess they just had more time on their hands to get things done back then—probably because they didn't waste half their lives sending goddamn texts or making goddamn vacuous phone calls.

That's something else I really like about Sylvia; she doesn't have a phone. Can you imagine that? She doesn't have a phone, I swear to God. She's an independent spirit, Sylvia. She doesn't run with the crowd. I love it when girls are independent like that. When they don't belong to a herd of their friends who have to like the same things and say the same things. Girls are like that, mostly. Boys are too, I think, but not to the same extent that girls are. You get a gang of girls together, and while they'd never say it, you just know that they're all scared to hell that the wrong thing might just slip out. It's a clever trick that girls can pull, really, looking carefree together and giggling and laughing and having fun, while all the time they are subconsciously monitoring every word that emerges as inane chatter from their sweet little mouths. How girls can do that I'll never know, I swear to God.

Sylvia says that people who carry phones around with them are slaves to them.

Actually, she says that they are slaves to anyone who happens to have their number, but I understand what she is getting at. At any rate, Sylvia likes to talk to people. Really talk, face to face, where you can look into someone's eyes and assess their body language.

I know exactly where Sylvia is coming from when she says that. She says that she loves intelligent conversation more than anything. Actually, so do I, and it's something that we very much have in common. There is something intimate about real conversation. Something about the sharing of ideas and the process of perhaps learning from someone else's ideas that is incredibly sensual. Most people just wouldn't get that. But Sylvia gets it; I see it in her eyes when we sit and talk together. And *I* certainly get it. I really do.

So Mom's put the phone down and she's turned to the counter and she's filling the coffee pot with water and she's taken a bag of coffee from a cupboard. And she hasn't said a word to me, like she's forgotten I'm here.

"Mom… What did you want?"

She turns and she almost seems startled.

"I wanted to make sure that you were okay."

She's using her *concerned-mom* voice. I don't mean to say that I think she's insincere, because that's the opposite of what I think. But she does have different voices that she uses for different reasons. I doubt that she knows she has them, these voices. But *I* know. And I always notice when she lapses into one of them. Like now.

"That's why I'm home early."

She walks over to the counter where I'm sitting and all the while she's inspecting my face. She reaches up like she wants to touch it, but I turn sharply away and her hand half drops.

"Your face is a little red. Looks like you've caught the sun. Have you had classes outside today?"

Now you could be too sharp here and wonder if she's trying to catch you out with a statement like that. It might panic you into wondering if she knows that you've not been at school. But I know Mom, and she just could not be that disingenuous with me. She really couldn't. So I just shake my head.

"No, just sitting out at break time, reading."

"Well, it looks like that swelling has gone down."

There's more she wants to say, I can tell. But I'm not going to help her; she's just going to have to come out and say it.

"I was talking to Jaqui today. At the office."

Here it comes.

"You know Jaqui? Jaqui Reynolds?"

Of course I know her. She's been to the house often enough. She's a partner at Mom's goddamn firm, for God's sake. Early forties but with great skin and fabulous blonde hair and dress sense to match. The kind of woman you'd just love to *just run your hands all over*, to use Eddie's parlance.

"Yeah Mom, I know Jaqui—if it's the same Jaqui who's been here a gazillion times. If it's the same Jaqui who's a partner at your firm. If it's the same…"

"Okay smart-ass."

That might sound harsh. But Mom is never harsh really. She's just letting me know that she's got the message. I *have* yanked her chain though. I always know how to do that. It cracks me up to see her react. I get a buzz out of it. I really do.

"Anyway, Jaqui says that if you are being bullied at school…"

"Christ, Mom. I'm not being bullied!"

I love my mom, but she does have a habit of doing this; sharing personal stuff with outsiders, and I hate her for it.

"You've no business talking about me to anyone, Mom. Jeez."

"Jaqui's not just anyone. She's known you since you were a baby. And anyway, I was worried."

"Well there's no need to worry. I'm not being bullied."

She looks at me for a moment. It's almost like she's wondering whether or not to believe me. It's ridiculous really, when I think of all the lies and half-truths that I have got past her over the years. I'm telling the truth here and she's questioning it. I'll never figure Mom out fully, I swear to God.

Her expression softens and I know she's not going to push it.

"Anyway, Jaqui says that if you *are* being bullied…"

Her raised hand pre-empts my reaction.

"...that I should go to see someone at the school right away."

"You'd better not do that, Mom..."

"Well, if you say you're not being bullied, then I won't. But you would tell me, wouldn't you? You wouldn't bottle it up inside?"

I sometimes think she's watched too many movies, too much television, when she comes out with crap like that. It's easiest to indulge her though. And she does mean well. She really does.

"Look, Mom, I'm fine, really I am. Don't do anything stupid like going to the school."

"Okay, I'll leave it for now. Since you say you're fine. But Jaqui was telling me about Westlands—you know, that school where she sends Eleanor."

"I'm not going to Westlands, Mom."

I've got to nip this idea in the bud.

"Eleanor really likes it there. And she's doing well. She's a year younger than you."

This is why I've got to nip this idea in the bud.

"I thought you were against private education."

An appeal to her sense of political morality.

"I *am* against it. But not to the point where I'd let it jeopardize your safety and well-being."

Okay, so now I know that Mom doesn't really *have* a sense of political morality. But then, very few people do. It's enough to make you puke, just looking at politicians for example. I hate politicians. Liars. I wouldn't believe politicians if they were telling me that day follows night. I really wouldn't. But this is Mom and I guess I love her so I'll try not to hold it against her. Like I say, she means well.

"Mom, I'm happy where I am. I'm doing okay and this is where my friends are."

"You do have friends then?"

"Of course I have friends."

Where the hell did that come from? The thing is, like I think I told you earlier, I don't really have friends. Unless I can count Sylvia. I wonder if I can. I've only known her for a few hours. But it feels like—and yes, get your barf bag ready—we're on the same wavelength.

"At Westlands you'd already know Eleanor. I'm sure she'd soon introduce you to her crowd."

I'm stunned at this. I really am. Eleanor is okay and everything. I've met her at parties and barbeques over the years and I guess we get along. But what the hell is Mom thinking? Well I know the answer to that, of course; Mom and Jaqui are always trying to throw old Eleanor and me together. But it's never going to happen. Do they really dream of some sort of dynastic coming together? Oh doesn't that just make you want to puke? And I have to say, it's out of character for Mom. For Jaqui—well, I wouldn't like to say.

And is it really so long since either of them were at school themselves? Since when did school kids ever start mixing with kids from the year below? If Mom wanted to see me being bullied, she couldn't engineer anything more guaranteed to do it than this. Like I said, old Eleanor is not a bad kid. And she's good looking too. And at social functions, sure we get on well enough. But at school? She's a year behind and therefore social poison. You know it. I know it. *What the hell are you thinking, Mom?* I should say something.

"So is that it? Do you feel better now?"

Mom looks at me. Her head tilts just a little to the left the way it always does when she's mulling something over.

"Well... If you say everything is okay...

It's only because I care so much. You know that."

"Sure I know, Mom. And this business about Westlands? We can forget about that, right?"

"It seems a shame. But if you're happy where you are… It's always an option though, will you remember that?"

"Sure Mom. But can I go now? I want to make some calls."

She picks up on that as quick as a flash. Like I said, she isn't stupid.

"To your friends?"

"Yeah, of course to my friends. Who did you think? The Secretary General of the UN?"

"Yes, that's funny Tom. Sarcasm is something they're teaching now?"

"Evidently they were teaching it back in your day too, Mom. Can I go now?"

"*May* I go, Tom, not *can* I go. A pity they don't spend less time on sarcasm and more time on grammar."

We're both smiling, not sniping at each other. One thing I love about Mom is that we can play these verbal games together and it never gets nasty or anything. We're quite close really, and I don't mind admitting it; I'm really fond of Mom. And I'm only saying this because so many guys at school seem to hate their parents. You listen to most kids and you'd think that it was like a war zone at home for them. I think that in a lot of cases, they just say things because they think it will make them sound cool.

That sure is true of Eddie. You listen to old Eddie at school and you'd think that him and his mom and dad were only one step removed from murder. You'd think that the atmosphere in their house would be spiky as a bed of nails, honest to God. But old Eddie, well he's nice and sweet and polite when he's at home. And Eddie's mom is lovely. She really is. And she can't do enough for Eddie and Helen. So it's only outside and at school that you see the hoodie-wearing Eddie. It's only outside and at school that you hear him trying to emulate the *patois* and speech patterns of South-Central LA. Like anyone would *ever* look at Eddie and believe for a moment that he was from *there*. But what the hell; I get the feeling that Eddie is going to make a super-fine lawyer or something very respectable one day. I really do.

I'm not saying that we don't have *any* rough kids from tough places at school; we sure as hell do. But I'd guess that for the most part the kids at school are like Eddie and me, however they want to play it. Perhaps they are not all as close with their parents as Mom and me are though. Who knows?

Anyway, I'm off the stool and I pick up my bag. It was nothing to worry about after all. I can tell myself all day long that I wasn't really worried in the first place, but I'd be lying. All kinds of stupid thoughts had been going through my goddamn head. You know it; I told you.

"I hope she's a sweet girl. You tell her I'm looking forward to meeting her someday."

Well that stops me.

"Oh come on, Tom. I was only guessing. Now I *know*. Who is she? What's her name? Does she go to your school?"

It's a bewildering barrage of questions. And I'm sucked into it. Does she know about Sylvia? How can she know? If she does, then she knows that I haven't been at school all day. And she knows I've been lying. What to say, what to say… And then it dawns on me. Mom doesn't know a goddamn thing. She's just fishing. And she's teasing me. Goddamn! Did I mention that moms can be bastards? Well mine can. She really can.

CHAPTER 6

Hanging on the telephone

I'm lying on my bed now. Looking around, I like the fact that I'm able to maintain the minimalist effect that I'm comfortable with. In fact, the room is like a good hotel room—at the Mondrian on Sunset Strip, say; it's light and the walls are smooth plaster painted white and there's fabulous wall-to-wall carpet. The furniture is all built-in and it's bleached mahogany. I have a walk-in, of course, but no en-suite. Only Mom and Dad's room has an en-suite, but the bathroom that I share with Madeleine is huge with fantastic chrome and glass and polished slate and mirrors and stuff. The shower is a glass-shrouded walk-in with jets that spray from the wall as well as overhead. It's a very impressive room. It really is.

But my room is cool too. It's totally devoid of visible clutter. Not even photographs. In fact, nothing that would personalize it in any way at all. I hate that, when people clutter up their houses like that, with crappy tasteless family snapshots in cheap frames on ill-matched furniture. And then they add to that the junk that they've collected or been given over an uneventful life. These things are supposed to be reminders of happy times—holidays or celebrations or God knows what. They say that these things remind them of this time or that, as if saying such crap can in any way validate having that tasteless crap surrounding them all the time. I mean, what kind of goddamn parent needs to be *reminded* what its kids look like? *Hello. Wake up in there. This is your son, Johnny, remember? Here, let me just take this picture you have on the mantelpiece and hold it against my face. There. Is that better? You remember me now?* Yeah, right. There are elderly people who are suffering from dementia or something where that might be reality for them, but I'm not talking about them. Just walk into most houses and somewhere I'll just bet you that you'll find photographs and other tasteless crap, just like I'm talking about. You know it.

But anyway, my room is not like that. I told you, it's like a hotel room if you really want to know. And I'm here lying on the bed and I'm a bit damp because I've taken a shower. I'm in a robe of course—I don't want to soak the sheets now do I? And the robe I'm wearing—well I'll tell you the label because I know you're just dying to know. It's actually a vintage Christian Dior robe that Madeleine got for me for my birthday last year. It's royal blue cotton velour with paisley trim on the cuffs and collar. Apparently, it was bought from some Hollywood stylist and was worn in a couple of movies. I don't know which ones, so there's no point asking. It's actually very comfortable, though I have to say that what I like best about it is the label. I mean, how many of *you* have vintage Dior in your wardrobes to use as day wear?

Seeing Red

So I'm lying on my bed and I'm turning my phone over in my hands. I want to push the numbers, but I'm hesitating. Obviously I want to speak to Sylvia. And I had tried earlier.

"Hello. Could I speak to Sylvia please?"

A pause and then an aggressive man's voice.

"No. You can't speak to goddamn Sylvia."

Not a stimulating dialogue, I think you'll agree. Not exactly up there with Socratic dialectic, for example. You can just imagine old Socrates there, sitting under a tree in ancient Athens, and his favorite pupil, Alcibiades wanders over to him.

"Socrates, noble teacher; today, may we discuss the nature of justice?"

"No, we goddamn can't."

Doesn't exactly have a ring to it, does it?

So I'm wondering if I dare call again. And that's a strange thing in itself, I think. Why shouldn't I just call? It's not like anyone can reach down the phone and grab me, like they can in cartoons. I like old cartoons—the Chuck Jones and Tex Avery Warner Brothers cartoons, the Hanna-Barbera *Tom and Jerry* cartoons. Those old slapstick cartoons slay me. They really do. Yet later on, Chuck Jones went on to do some *Tom and Jerry* cartoons and you can tell them straight away when you watch them because they are just not funny. Not the least little bit. I can never figure that out myself; Chuck Jones was fantastic with *Bugs Bunny* and *Road Runner* and stuff. But he screwed up *Tom and Jerry* good.

So what the hell, I punch in the numbers anyway and lie back listening to the ringing tone.

"Who is it?"

"Can I speak to Sylvia please?"

"SYLVIA! PHONE!"

I hate that, when someone bellows out like that. I'm getting a mental picture of some unshaven slob of a guy wearing a dirty vest, stuffing food into his greasy face while he can't take his eyes off the TV. I'm figuring that this must be Sylvia's dad, and this is the unflattering picture I have of him. We all do that though; make pictures of people we're speaking to on the phone, I mean, if we've never seen them in real life. I always imagine women to be super cool and funky and sexy, for example. Unless they have those really miserably obviously middle-aged voices that some women have. I mean, sometimes you just know that the person you're talking to is dowdy and frumpy and miserable enough to strip the blossom from the trees with just a glance. It makes me puke to think of that. Not really old people, I'm not talking about them. Really old people have these croaky voices and you can tell right away when you listen to them that they're really old. Actually, I like old people. They tend to be far less judgmental than middle-aged people. I guess it's because old people have come to know exactly who they are, while middle-aged people are still bitter about the fact that they don't measure up to the person they saw themselves becoming in their youth. An old person once told me that, and you have to admit that it is the truth. It really is.

"Hello?"

I've been daydreaming with the phone pressed against my ear, so the voice on the line comes as a surprise.

"Sylvia?"

What a stupid thing for me to say. Of course it's Sylvia; her voice is soft and sweet and immediately reminds me of the gentle sound of that brook we were sitting next to just a few hours earlier.

"Holden?"

I'm not going to rise to that. I'm not going to make an issue of it because if I do I just know that she'll rag me about it forever. So I don't say anything, but there isn't an awkward pause or anything.

"I didn't really think you'd call."

"Really? Why not?"

Yeah, really, why not? Why wouldn't she think I'd call? I took her number. I said I'd call. And here I am, calling.

"Well, sometimes people say they'll call just to be polite."

She's right of course. I've done that myself. Said I'd call someone just as a convenient way of getting rid of them when I'd no intention of calling them. I remember this one time, a few years ago. I went to this tennis camp in the summer—as if I was ever going to have any kind of athletic prowess—but anyway, there was another kid there who was just as crap as me, and we became kinda friends for the duration. When it was time to go home, we swapped numbers and said we'd stay in touch and everything. But I didn't really mean it. I mean, we had nothing in common other than being rubbish at tennis. But this kid meant it; he called night after night, and I kept getting Mom to make excuse after excuse. It began to wear Mom out and she said she wasn't going to lie for me anymore. This bugged me for a while, but the next time this kid rang, Madeleine answered and she just told him straight out that I didn't want to talk to him. Straight out, just like that. I guess she was being honest, but I can imagine that kid being crestfallen. Still, I expect he's got over it now. It *has* been a few years.

"Well it's not in my nature to be polite, so here I am, calling."

She laughs. It's a sweet laugh and I immediately picture her head tilting back slightly, her black hair tumbling from her neck, those straight, white teeth. And for a moment my breathing is very shallow.

"God, Holden, you're the most polite person I've ever met. You're such a gentleman."

Now if most people were to say that to you, you'd shudder, because you'd know that what they were actually saying, whether meaning it or not, was that you were not the least bit cool. Why that should matter

I don't really know, but it does. It really does. And you know it as well as I do. But Sylvia saying it, it just comes out like a compliment. And you know that that's just how she meant it too.

"Well, that's as maybe. But I don't want to talk about that; I'm calling about what you said earlier today. About going to see a movie sometime."

I can be like that on the phone. More often than not, I am. Actually, I don't much like talking on the phone to tell you the truth. There's something really phoney about talking on the phone if you ask me, and no, that isn't a pun. You can't see the other person and they could be stringing you along, bored, or even just downright lying, and if they're cunning at it you'd never really know.

"You really want to go?"

You know, I've said this often but I can't help repeating myself; girls are exasperating!

"Yes, I really want to go. What, did you think that I was calling just to tell you I'd changed my mind? When did you last get a call like that?"

The laugh again. God, it's cute as hell when she's being coy like this.

"I'm more used to not getting calls at all."

Is she fishing for a compliment here? Am I supposed to tell her that she's so gorgeous that I can't believe that guys aren't calling her all the time? Or some crap like that at any rate? Or is she just stating a fact? See what I mean about girls? This is the sort of thought process every guy has to go through when he's talking to a girl. How can you ever possibly understand what they want?

"Sure. Poor little you. So what night were you thinking of going?"

I'm taking a risk being so off-hand with her, but I feel confident that she'll know that I don't mean anything by it.

"Oh. I hadn't thought… I don't suppose…"

I'm waiting.

"I don't suppose you're free on Friday?"

Obviously she *had* thought. She's coming across all insecure again, like she did down in the woods when she first suggested that we might go see a movie together. She's putting this on, surely.

"Well actually…"

"It doesn't matter. Another day…"

"Hey, let me finish. I was going to say that actually, Friday would be just fine. What do you want to see?"

Well this is where my heart is sinking. I'm waiting to hear just what it is I'm going to have to sit through. At the moment the big things are *blockbuster film part three*, *summer-smash part two* and *you-loved-it-the-first-time-now-let's-milk-it-for-all-it's-worth part six*. I can't actually remember all the names of these movies but I'm sure you get the idea. I read about filmmakers whinging from time to time about how Hollywood is run by accountants these days and no one ever takes a risk on original talent. I guess the current line-up now showing backs that up. I hate sequels. I really do.

"Well, there's a movie at the Bijou-Roxy…"

Now I'm interested. The Bijou-Roxy is a restored theater at the edge of town. The interior is very plush, and the staff are all in uniform, and there are heavy velvet drapes everywhere and the seats are deep and plush. Did I say how plush it is? I could go on, but suffice to say it's an incredible place. Even more incredible is that it shows art house films, experimental stuff that the big chains just won't run.

Accountants eh? Who the hell needs them? I like experimental stuff. I'm bored to death with the standard Hollywood three-act potboiler. Not that Hollywood is all like that, despite what the filmmakers say.

Some fantastic and original and creative stuff comes out of Hollywood.

The Bijou-Roxy also has a habit of showing movies from history that you'd never otherwise get to see on a big screen. I saw Alan Ladd and Veronica Lake in a classic black and white film there once. *This Gun for Hire* it was called, and it was fantastic. Watching them play their parts up there, on that big screen, it was like going back in time, I swear to God. I don't know what's showing at the Bijou-Roxy right now, but it won't be mindless blockbuster stuff, that's for sure.

"What's showing?"

I ask in anticipation now. Yes of course I'm genuinely interested. I really am.

"*Lawrence of Arabia.*"

"Okay. So what time shall I pick you up?"

I'm pretty casual as I say that. But

actually, you know what? I'm quite excited. Really, I am.

"It starts at eight. So is seven okay?"

She's using that little girl voice again, the one she uses when she's not confident of the response she's going to get. She used it back down in the woods when she asked if I wanted her number, like I said. To be honest, I don't know whether it *is* a lack of confidence. She probably knows that it sounds just as cute as hell. She can probably sense how shallow my breathing is down the goddamn phone. Girls are perceptive like that. I'm not even saying that they do it on purpose either. I just think it's a genetic thing. Girls have everything that it could possibly take to manipulate guys. They're born that way, just the same as they're born with arms and legs. And every girl knows how to use what she's got. Even the girls that don't know what they've got, they can wrap guys around their little fingers. They do it naturally. They can't help it. It's in their natures. And you know what? Guys love them for that. We really do, honest to

God. Any wonder that most of the time when girls get together they spend half their time laughing at guys? Madeleine told me that, and I've never doubted it.

"Yeah, seven is fine."

"Great. See you around, then."

"Yeah, see you around."

The phone goes dead and I'm left holding the receiver. Sylvia really doesn't like telephones. I mean, I can't stand the thought of jabbering on all day myself, but that was a bit abrupt, even for me. Still, what do I care? I know that Sylvia means nothing by it. And besides, *Lawrence of Arabia...*

Now I'm betting a lot of people nowadays have no idea what *Lawrence of Arabia* is. Well let's just start by saying that it is the greatest film ever made. And in case you're about to sneer and wonder just what a sixteen year-old kid would know about great movies, let me tell you that it's not just me saying it. Steven Spielberg says it. And I'm thinking that even *you* would agree that old Steven might know a thing or two about films, right? I read somewhere that Steven Spielberg makes a point of watching *Lawrence of Arabia* before he starts work on any new movies. The photography is breathtaking—I'm reduced to clichés describing it, so you can imagine how special it must be, right? Those incredible views of the desert. The shimmering heat. And the director lets us linger on those views, gives us time to let it all sink in.

I hate the way that in modern films, well the goddamn camera is just moving all the time so you don't know where you're supposed to be looking *from*, and half the time you don't know what you are supposed to be looking *at*. Actually, Steven Spielberg is pretty much to blame for that—although an honorable mention goes to Orson Welles with *Citizen Kane*. The camera moving all over the place is pretty much a Spielberg trademark. And because he was so successful with it, every talentless hack has followed him. Trouble is, only a few directors can do that with any panache—Robert Zemekis is another one—and everything else looks cheap and stylized and phony.

And you know what I hate the most? There's a particular shot that's used a lot and if you see it when you're watching a movie you know you might as well switch off or walk out because it says, clear as a bell, that the director is a cheap hack. You'll know the one; it's where the camera is looking at something in a room; and then the camera starts to move back so we can see more of the room; and then, as if by magic—are we supposed to gasp at this point?—the camera has backed right out of the window and we can see the house. Then it moves back some more and we can see the house and the garden, and it's rising up now, so that we can see the house and the garden from above. Then it goes back even more and even higher until we can see the whole goddamn neighborhood. At this point of course, anyone with any artistic discernment at all is reaching for a barf bag. It makes you want to puke, that shot does. No top-notch director would ever use it. Only hacks and phonies. Sometimes, to show creative variety, they do it the other way round. Oh how I gasp with wonder when they do that. Start way out and bring the camera in until it's inside the house and forcing us to look at something dim-witted. There are far more hacks and phonies than there are artists. And that one shot proves it. I swear to God.

I'm pondering all this when my door opens, startling me a bit. I hate that—when I'm deep in thought and someone brings me out of it pretty sharp. It's like being woken up in the middle of a particularly fantastic dream. Madeleine pokes her head in the door. Good thing that I'm decent.

"For Chrissakes, Maddie!"

I make out that I"m annoyed—and I"d have every right to be—but really I'm not. I am totally in favor of having my privacy, but Madeleine is a special case. And besides, right away, I can see that she is unhappy about something.

"Sorry. I wasn't sure if you were here or not.'

I *could* suggest that a good way to find out would be to knock. But Madeleine seems like she has something on her mind so I let it go.

"Well, I guess I *am* here. So what did you want?"

She's still outside the door, and usually she would have breezed right in. I can tell that something is wrong, but Madeleine and me, we know each other well enough not to pry.

"Oh nothing. I was just bored and wondered if you were watching TV or something."

Of course that is a dead give away that she has something on her mind, but I'm going to let it go for now.

"Well, I was just about to."

I pick up the remote lying next to me and hit the button. I have configured it so that the TV starts in mute-mode, so it doesn't freak out the whole house when I switch it on. Sometimes, if I wake up in the middle of the night, I switch on my TV. You can imagine how it would go down with Mom and Dad if there was a blast of noise at three a.m. or something.

"Are you coming in?"

Madeleine smiles, which gives me a lift, I admit it, and before you know it, she's lying next to me on my bed. She's wearing just the Versace jeans and a Stella McCartney T-shirt and her long legs seem to stretch to the end of the bed.

We lie like this for a while, chatting away about nothing in particular with the TV on in the background, unwatched. There's something on Madeleine's mind for sure, but she isn't going to say anything, so I chill back and talk about clothes and shoes and make-up and stuff with her. We can fill hours with talk like that. And I comment on the polish on her toenails, perfect as always. I guess that it's from the OPI Hollywood Collection, and that the shade is *I'm Not Really a Waitress*.

Seeing Red

It cracks me up that OPI has these really cute names for their stuff. It really does. And it cracks Madeleine up that I know so much about stuff like this, which is why I commented on it in the first place. Why she should be surprised though, I don't really know. After all, she is the one who taught me all about this stuff.

If you want to know the truth, it is just an educated guess I've made about the nail polish, based on the color and the fact that I know that Madeleine buys a lot of OPI stuff. But it seems to make her happy for a while, so that makes me happy.

And now we are just sitting here watching reruns of old black and white episodes of *The Beverly Hillbillies*. We both enjoy them and Madeleine spots Sharon Tate in one of the episodes, which gives her a buzz, even though it's a goddamn shame what happened to Sharon Tate, being murdered with her unborn baby by the Charles Manson gang and all.

Whatever is troubling Madeleine, I guess she'll tell me when she feels she wants to.

CHAPTER 7

I'd rather be dreaming...

I wake up and it's the middle of the night. My TV is switched off and the lights are off, but I'm still lying on my bed wrapped inside the Dior robe. There's a space next to me because Madeleine has gone. Yes, of course she's gone. We're not in the habit of sleeping together, sicko. That would be appalling.

I twist my head to look at the glowing numbers on the bedside clock. It's three in the morning. I don't feel sleepy at all so I reach for the TV remote but something stops me. I can hear someone sobbing. And I listen harder and I know it's from the next room. Madeleine's room.

There's nothing I hate more in the whole world than the thought that someone I care about is unhappy. And I don't just *care* about Madeleine; it goes deeper than that. There was definitely something on her mind earlier. Now I'm wishing I'd come straight out and asked her, but you can never turn back the clock.

I am still wearing my robe so I creep out onto the landing. It's definitely Madeleine. I wonder if I should go to see what the matter is. Would she want me to see her crying like that? Probably not, but it's too late because I'm already tapping on the door as loud as I dare. She's definitely heard me because the sobbing stops immediately. I know that she knows it's me; Mom or Dad would have just barged in.

"Maddie—it's me."

I'm hissing the words. God I hate whispering. Even the sound of other people whispering makes my skin crawl. Some people can't stand the sound of chalk on a blackboard. I can. I can listen to *that* all day. But whispering—it makes me want to commit acts of violence. It really does, I swear to God. I just can't stand it.

So here I am, whispering and hating the sound and hating myself, but it's for Madeleine so I grit my teeth. And she doesn't reply and there's only quiet from beyond that door. So I have to hiss again.

"Maddie, come on..."

And then the door clicks open and through the two-inch gap (I'm guessing but it couldn't be much more) I can see Madeleine standing in those cute Tiffany Blue pajamas. I can barely see her face but what I can see are tear tracks down her cheeks and an eye that is swollen and red.

"Maddie, what's wrong?"

I barely notice that I'm hissing now.

"Nothing."

"Then why are you crying? Aren't you going to let me in?"

I realize that standing on the landing pleading to get into my sister's bedroom— well, it must seem like a redneck courtship, but really, what else can I do?

"Come on Maddie, it's obviously something. You can tell me about it, you know that."

But already I know that she's not going to tell me anything at all. Not right now. She'll have to tell me something at some point though. I already know that there *is* something wrong. And she knows that I know. I won't let it go until I know that she is going to be all right. That's the way it works when you care about someone. I know that and she knows that. And you know it too, don't you? It's a universal law.

"No, not right now. Just leave me alone. I'll talk to you tomorrow."

Well, there's not a lot I can say to that. She closes the door on me and I hear it click. She'll talk to me tomorrow, so I'll have to wait until then. But my mind is racing all the same, and it keeps coming back to just one thing. A boy.

When girls cry like that, there's pretty much always a boy involved. Madeleine has a boyfriend—David Lloyd. He's a year older than her, twenty, and they've been seeing each other for about a year. Actually, he's a pretty cool guy and we get along really well. I love the Porsche 911 Carrera that he drives—yes, his family has money all right. But right now, I'm thinking that if he's done anything to hurt my sister, I just want to tear his arms and legs off. And this is what I'm thinking as I eventually drift into sleep. And that's another reason to hate David Lloyd; I *should* have been dreaming of Sylvia.

CHAPTER 8

No one to talk to

Another sunny day wasted at school. All I've done is look out of the classroom windows all day. I can see the athletics fields and stuff, and all that green makes me think of yesterday and being with Sylvia in the woods and by the brook.

Of course the school wanted to know where I'd been yesterday and I just told them I'd felt sick and gone home. I said that in case anyone had noticed me in the library. And because of what happened with Eddie, some dumb-ass kid may have said something about seeing me before the bell. So I made this stuff up about being sick and forgetting the note from my mom. There is no such note of course, and I'll have to forge one tonight to bring in tomorrow. I've done it before and it has never failed, so I'm not stressed about it.

I hung around the yard when I got here this morning, looking out for Sylvia, but she never showed. I have to say that I was very disappointed. Really, I was. I thought about cutting school again and going down to that brook, as if she'd be there again. But I'm smart enough to realize just what a stupid romantic fantasy that is. I just hate people who live their lives as though things should be how they *want* them to be and not the way they *really* are. People like that are just deluded morons, and it's because reality has a habit of intruding on their romantic notions that they are so easily rendered unhappy.

All I want to do now, really, is just sit here, staring out of the window, thinking about Sylvia and that incredible laugh she has and her hair and her smile. And the scars on the inside of her arm. What the hell is that all about? I want to spend all my time thinking about Sylvia, for sure. But I can't. Because there is also Madeleine. I'm worried sick about Madeleine. She said she'd talk to me today, but I didn't see her this morning—which is very unusual—so I guess I'll have to wait until I get home. I'm hoping it's nothing. Girls can get weepy about things sometimes. It just makes me mad and sad to see girls getting upset. It breaks my heart, it really does.

So this is how I spend my Thursday, daydreaming until the last bell. I don't think I've spoken more than a dozen words the whole day. I've been in my own world. Even Eddie has been ignoring me. Not a word, not even a scowl. I wonder if he's cooling down and realizing that I'm *not* perving after his kid sister. It would be nice to think that things could get back to normal with old Eddie, but it's not the most important thing on my mind as I sit alone on the bus home.

When I get home the driveway is clear, so Mom's not back and I'll be able to talk to Madeleine. But the house is as empty as the drive. No Mom. No Dad. No Madeleine. So I shower and change, and I lie in my room and I wonder where they are, the two most important girls in my life right now.

I've been lying here for an hour or so, turning my phone over between my fingers. I'm wondering whether I should call them, find out where they are, how they are doing. I haven't as yet, because I'm disturbed by how strong the feeling is for me to do this. It makes me seem needy somehow. I don't find that an attractive quality when I notice it in others and I sure as hell don't want to find it in myself. But before you know it, I'm hitting the speed dial for Madeleine's cell phone. It rings and it rings and then after some mechanical clicking, there she is.

"Hi. You've reached Maddie's phone. I'm not talking to you right now because I'm either not available or I just don't like you. Feel free to leave a message after the beep. Or don't, as the case may be. Maybe I'll get back to you, maybe I won't. No guarantees." She sounds cool in the message, but I know that Madeleine would just *love* you to leave a message. She'd hate to think she'd missed out on *anything*.

I listen to Maddie's message all the way through, even though I've heard it plenty of times before, just because I'm comforted by the sound of her voice. I don't leave a message of my own though. I can't imagine where Maddie might be, but I don't dwell on that; not when I can be calling Sylvia.

I don't have Sylvia's number assigned to a speed-dial button yet, so I have to browse through the phone's address book to find it. I find it and press enter. It rings and it rings.

"Who the hell is that?"

Right away I'm thinking of the slob again, the slob I imagine to be Sylvia's dad. I can hear the sound of a television blaring in the background this time, which only reinforces the image I've created.

"Can I speak to Sylvia please?"

"Christ, another one of you. She's not here."

And the phone is slammed down. And I'm just holding my own phone against my ear. I'm not shocked at the rudeness—come on, you know me better than that. I'm just wondering what he meant. Another one of you. Another boy? Is Sylvia seeing someone? A gazillion possible scenarios are racing through my head—most of them ones that I do not like at all.

I have to tell myself that I have only known Sylvia for a day, so it shouldn't matter. But it goddamn does matter. It really does, and I hate myself because it does. Why the hell can't Madeleine be home? Christ, even Mom or Dad or both would be better than the empty house right now. Goddamn girls. It's absolutely impossible to like girls, I swear to God.

And I just know that I am going to continue ranting to myself like this and making myself feel worse and worse, when the little miracle happens. I hear a car pull into the driveway, and before you know it, the front door opens and closes again. Mom's home.

I throw on some cotton Dockers and a Ralph Lauren Polo shirt and go down to greet her. I find her in the kitchen. She lives in the kitchen.

"Hi. I didn't think anyone was home. None of the lights are on."

And that's true. I hadn't thought about it, but I've been lying upstairs for ages and while it isn't really dark, we're certainly well into dusk.

"I've just been lying in my room, doing some reading for school and watching TV."

I can lie as casually as that any time I need to. It doesn't do any harm and it gives Mom no reason to ask any questions.

"Have you eaten anything? Do you want me to fix something for you?" She's saying this as she's making herself a cup of coffee and not really looking at me.

"No, I'm fine. I had a burger and fries at the mall on my way home."

"Oh, so you were at the mall. Buy anything nice?"

She still isn't looking at me but she is at least interested now. She likes to see the clothes that Madeleine and I buy. She's a *fashionista* herself, is Mom.

"No, I was just looking... Do you know what time Maddie will be back tonight?"

It's worth asking; she just might know, if Madeleine has spoken to her over breakfast this morning.

"She might not be back at all. She was going to spend the day with Kirsty. Then they were going out tonight. She said she might stay over. Why, do you need her for something?"

Jeez, Mom. If you want to pry, at least try to disguise it a little. I *want* to say that, but I don't.

"No, nothing important. I just wondered where everyone was tonight."

"Well, your father is having dinner with clients. He said, remember?"

I don't remember, but I don't say anything.

"And I'm going to have to shut myself in the study. I've got tons to do, so you'll have to entertain yourself this evening."

Now she turns to look at me.

"Will you be all right on your own?"

This is too much. It's not like I'm five years old or anything.

"Mom, I'm not five. Give me a break. I'm going back to my room."

"I know. Sometimes I forget though. You'll always be my little boy, Tom."

Oh, I can't even look at her when she's coming out with drivel like this and I turn away in disgust. If she wasn't my mother...

"I'm going."

"Well, I'm going to be busy in the study. It's really important that I get this work done before tomorrow, so don't disturb me unless the house is on fire, okay?"

I can only shake my head as I turn to head back to my room.

"Sure, Mom. If the house is on fire."

As I climb the stairs, I wonder just what the nature of this work might be. She does this from time to time—locks herself in the study and asks not to be disturbed. Sometimes she's on her own and sometimes she's in there with Dad. And that's strange because I can't see them in there working together. They are in totally different businesses. And I have my suspicions. I have been into their study when I've been home alone, and I've fired up their computer. And I'll tell you, what I found in the history drop-down of their web browser actually shocked me. No really, it did.

Sometimes I think I'm still traumatized by it. They visit sites for swingers. I guess that's an old-fashioned term, but I like it better than wife-swappers. I can't be certain that they go through with it, but something tells me that they do. There *are* Saturday nights now and then when they go out and stay out overnight. It isn't often, but what do you think? Yeah, I think so too. I wonder if Eddie would think of them as goddamn perverts.

CHAPTER 9

You can't compete with a movie star

Friday nights are noisy. Especially in the part of town around the Bijou-Roxy. I guess it's late—well, it's just eleven-thirty at any rate—so the streets are bound to be full of weekend party animals. And now of course there is us; all of us who have just spilled out of the theater.

I'm holding Sylvia's hand and while people are filing past us and bustling around us, I barely notice them. We are not speaking. Sylvia is like me and she likes to savor the rich beauty of what we have just seen. *Lawrence of Arabia*. The blue sky. The golden sand. Peter O'Toole. I have to say that it's taken my breath away to see it like that, up on the big screen. It really has.

There are a million cafes and bars around here and all with tables and chairs outside. It's a very bohemian part of the city if you really want to know. It isn't so long ago that it was totally seedy and run down. But over the years, it's gentrified. The big old houses have gradually been bought up and restored, mostly by creative types and, inevitably, by lawyers. But it's the creative types who give this area its character—advertising people, designers and so on. Lawyers don't give character to anything; they just suck the soul from everything they touch. It's a fact, it really is. Dad owns two properties around here that he's had converted to apartments and rents out, so you see what I mean.

I don't want to go home. It is great being with Sylvia. I just totally love the softness of her fingers closed gently around mine, and when I consciously think about it, I can feel my chest tighten and I can feel every individual beat of my heart, I swear to God. And even watching the movie, just feeling her pressed against me, and the times that her head rested on my shoulder—God that was amazing.

I'm sounding corny, like some gushing idiot from those trash romance novels and TV movies and I'm not like that really, as you surely know. All the same, Sylvia does have an effect on me. She really does.

"Would you like a coffee?"

I'm not talking; it's Sylvia. I've just been luxuriating in how the film has made me feel, and the atmosphere of this part of town and the sights and sounds and smells.

"Sure. Where do you want to go?"

"There's a little place down there, just off the main road."

She's pointing to a pedestrianized alleyway just off the main drag. It's a little darker than here, but it's not dingy, and the alleyway is broad and there are little coffee shops and restaurants on either side.

Sylvia takes me straight to a place that she's obviously been to before and I find myself wondering if I'm the first boy to sit across from her at an outside table. The thing is, I'm pretty sure I know the answer to that, and I'm certain that you do too, right? Right. And I'm wondering if she was here last night, even, when I couldn't get to speak to her on the phone.

Cindy, our waitress, brings coffee to the table and sets it down without spilling a drop. I'll be giving Cindy a good tip when we leave for that. I absolutely hate it when you get coffee slopping out of the cup and into the saucer because some wannabe actress/waitress doesn't take the trouble to care about the job she's doing now. I guess guys can be as bad, but I'm a teenage boy—I tend to choose places where there are cute girls waiting on the tables.

Still, I only have eyes for Sylvia tonight. She's wearing a cotton summer dress that hangs from her shoulders with two string straps. It's white with a printed pattern of large, pink rose blooms. When she's standing, you can see that it's short so that only someone with long, toned legs would ever dare to wear it. And all night long I've noticed that Sylvia has long, toned legs. And she's wearing these flip-flops that have been designed to seem like they're sort of Japanese—all straw and black cotton—that make the cutest slap-slap-slap sound as she walks.

"I tried to call you last night."

I don't know why I'm saying this. I guess it's been bugging me that she wasn't home and I'm driving myself crazy wondering where she actually was. I know, I know, that's not the least bit cool. But I'm being honest with you, right? Actually, it's not the thought of *where* she was; it's *who* she might have been with.

"Oh, I was out last night."

And that's all she says. It's obvious she doesn't want to say more than that and although I'm just dying to ask her for details, I manage to let it go. Instead, I pick up one of her hands and I'm inspecting her fingers.

I can see the scars running up the inside of her right forearm. It's great, the way she's not self-conscious about them. Strangely, exposed like this, they don't seem quite so dramatic. And I'm looking at her long slender fingers.

"You've got beautiful nails. Don't you ever wear nail polish?"

"Do you think I need to?"

Normally, with a girl, a question like that would need to be answered very carefully, but I'm already comfortable enough with Sylvia not to be phased by it.

I shake my head.

"You don't need to. I just think that it would look good."

"I don't have the money to waste on stuff like that. We're not *all* Hathaways."

Now that sounds like something of a rebuff, but it's not. She's smiling as she says it.

"Well, I could bring you some. I know what would look really good on you."

She laughs out loud—that tinkling, sweet laugh that sends tingles down my arms—and she pulls her hand away to cover her mouth so that my heart jumps at the sheer loveliness of the gesture.

"Are you gay or something?"

She doesn't mean anything by it and I realize that it's a fair question. I mean, how many boys *do* know anything about girlie make-up and stuff and *aren't* gay? I doubt there are many. So I smile right back at her, shaking my head.

"I have an older sister. We're always looking at fashion and make-up and stuff. Sometimes I even paint her nails for her. I'm actually quite accomplished at it."

This is true, and I can see that Sylvia is genuinely fascinated.

"I could paint your nails if you want."

She thinks about this for a moment.

"Sure. Why not? You could come back to my house tomorrow if you like…"

She's gone all coy and hesitant, the way she does when she's fishing for something she'd really like but not sure that she's going to get it.

Tomorrow is Saturday and I'm not doing anything in particular. And I honestly can't think of anything I'd rather be doing than spending time with Sylvia.

"Sure. That would be fine."

At least I know that tomorrow she'll be with me.

We're drinking our coffee some more, and I pick up her hand again. I look up and I can see that she is aware of me looking at the scars on her arm.

"Aren't you ever going to ask me?"

I know what she is talking about, and I shrug.

"I don't suppose I was, no."

And that's true. I'm aching with curiosity for sure, but it's her business and I can imagine that it's something very personal and serious.

"But since you've brought it up, then tell me. I won't pretend that I'm not interested."

She pulls back her hand and she's looking me right in the eye and she holds me with her gaze, so that I momentarily stop breathing.

"I cut myself."

I think I'd guessed that for myself. You don't get track scars like that by accident. But she doesn't say anything more than that.

"Why?"

"I don't know. Stress. Boredom."

She's gazing past me now. She seems distant somehow, like her mind is altogether elsewhere. People can do that—I'm sure that we've all done it at some time. But I'm engaged in this conversation now, so I bring her back.

"You're too smart to be bored. Only idiots allow themselves to be bored."

That brings her back all right.

"Are you saying that I'm an idiot?"

"Not at all. I just can't imagine you letting yourself succumb to boredom is what I mean. I just think that you'd always be able to find something to occupy you."

She's holding me with that gaze again. God, it's so intense when she does that.

"I *did* find something. I cut myself."

I shrug and say nothing. What can I say? We're in territory that I don't understand. I could jabber on and dig myself into a hole, but I'm smart enough not to travel down that particular path.

"Doesn't it hurt?"

I can't imagine that it doesn't, so I truly want to know. I mean, let's face it, most of us would run a million miles to avoid pain. I really can't see why anyone would bring it upon themselves. I really can"t.

"You feel it at first. When the blade begins to slice through the top layer of your skin."

You know, I can't believe I'm really sitting here listening to this. She's sitting there, saying these words and you can bet your life that anyone just passing by and seeing us would imagine that we're just making innocent small talk. But she's just rubbing her fingertips, slowly and gently along the length of one of her scars while she fixes me with that gaze and continues to explain. And I'm just thinking of biology lessons with old Jackson. I'm thinking of those diagrams in the books where you see a cross section of the skin—epidermis, dermis and all those nerve cells. And I see those nerve cells shrieking out to the old brain up there to put a stop to it all.

"It's when you see the blood oozing out and that's all you can look at. You see it trickle over your arm. You watch where it runs. And you don't feel anything after that. You're just watching these little rivers running slowly over your arm and you're trying to predict the patterns that they make. It's like some psychedelic show that consumes your attention. And before you know it, you're moving the knife, deeper and further, until that's all there is. You're just seeing red."

Well, she's saying it and I'm hearing it and I don't know if I can quite comprehend it without feeling a little bit sick. I take her arm and I'm still held by her gaze as I gently trace the path of these scars with my fingertips.

"I haven't done it for more than a year now."

"Was it hard to stop?"

I ask because the way she's describing it, it sounds like an addiction, like smoking or drinking or God knows what else. She shakes her head.

"No. I just haven't done it in over a year is what I'm saying."

"So life has been fulfilling and stress-free for this last year then. That's good."

I don't believe that myself as I'm saying it, but I want her to tell me more. I think she's holding something back. She shakes her head again, but she's not smiling or making light of it like you'd think she might if she wanted the subject to change. There's more to her life, that's for sure. And right now I just want to reach across the table and hold her and tell her that everything will be all right, even if I don't know how I can possibly guarantee such a thing. But I continue to stroke the scars on her arm, limp in my hands, until I'm tracing the scars that spell out *Tom*.

"Just one more thing."

She's all attention and there's a hint of a smile in her eyes again, which pleases me no end.

"What made you do *this*?"

She's puzzled for a moment until she realizes that I am referring to the letters that spell out my name in pink scar tissue. Then she pulls back her arm and laughs, covering her mouth with her hand—God, am I *ever* going to stop loving the way that she does that?

"Oh my God, you didn't think... ? You *did* didn't you?"

She's laughing even more now and I still love that laugh even though it's obvious that she's laughing at me. I can handle being laughed at by a girl; I have an older sister, don't I?

"It's okay, Tom. I haven't had a secret crush on you."

She laughs again. Why would she think I wouldn't have been pleased to hear that she'd been secretly wanting me? Makes me more convinced than ever that I am right not to tell her that I've secretly liked *her* for years.

"So who's Tom then?"

She takes my hands in hers and leans towards me.

"Tom Cruise. I *did* used to have a crush on *him*."

Tom Cruise. Well that's not so crushing; I mean, how could I compete with a movie star?

And then we're walking down the suburban streets of a suburban neighborhood and the coffee shop is far behind us. I did leave Cindy a good tip, just in case you are wondering.

We're walking slowly, hand in hand beneath the street lights, and it's quiet. All you can hear is the click of my Armani shoes on the sidewalk and the slap-slap-slap of her sweet little flip-flops. This is a part of town where Sylvia lives and while it seems okay enough, it's a million miles removed from the suburbs where I live. The houses are smaller and closer together and they all look the same. It all seems pleasant enough though, I suppose. We reach a small gate where a short path leads from the street to the front door.

"This is me."

We stand by the gate for just a moment and I wonder whether Sylvia is going to invite me in for a coffee or something. I really truly hope that she will. I'm kind of sad that the evening is coming to a close, if you really want to know.

But she opens the gate and she doesn't let go of my hand as she starts up the path. I walk with her, still hoping.

We're standing on the doorstep, facing each other for a moment that is not in the least bit awkward but is—to use a trashy romance novel cliché—pregnant with expectation. I can't believe I just said that, I really can't. All the same, I'm just standing here and wanting nothing more than to hold her and kiss her. I swear to God, if that could just happen it's all I want in the whole world.

"Did you have a good time tonight?"

She's asking me.

"Sure. Yeah, I had a great time. It was a great choice of movie."

"It was just the movie that made it good?"

She's fishing again, but she's not hesitant and coy this time. And it's like some magnetism is pulling us together and we're in each other's arms and I feel her soft lips pressing gently against mine. This is what I truly want and it is a beautiful moment, it really is. I mean, truly wonderfully beautiful. Her lips are slightly moist and warm and I can taste the coffee on her breath. She's giving herself to me in this kiss, in this moment, and she kisses like this kiss is all that matters in the entire world. And for me, it is.

And then there is shouting and yelling coming from inside the house, a man and a woman. Sylvia breaks away from me and for a brief moment I see fear in her eyes. I am bewildered for a second as I get my bearings—I was totally lost in that kiss.

"Christ, I'd better go."

Sylvia says this even as she turns from me and fumbles in her bag for her key. Before I can say anything, she has the key in the lock and she's swinging the door open so that the yelling is clear and present. Sylvia starts to step inside then turns quickly back to me.

"I'm sorry, Tom. It's been a lovely evening but I have to go. I'll see you tomorrow."

And next thing you know, I'm standing on the doorstep looking at the door that has slammed in my face. The yelling continues and now I hear Sylvia's voice and she's obviously trying to calm things down in there.

I want to bang on the door; I want to be in there, making sure that Sylvia is okay. But I don't do anything. I feel like a snooper listening in as I stand there. And I do stand there for a full minute or two until it seems that things are calming down. And I realize that I can't just stand there all night, so I turn and head for home.

Now there is only the click of my shoes on the pavement, though in my head I can hear the slap of Sylvia's flip-flops. All I can think of is Sylvia. And more than anything, I'm thinking of what she told me, about her cutting herself. And I'm imagining the blade in her hand. I'm imagining the skin parting and the blood beginning to flow along her arm. And I can't stop thinking about this until all I see is the blood; and I'm seeing red.

CHAPTER 10

Why can't life be simple?

By the time I get home, there isn't a car on the road. My leafy suburb is quiet—which is pretty much what you'd expect given the time. It is one-thirty in the morning after all.

I've walked home and it's taken me an hour. And all the time I've been thinking of Sylvia. I can't stop thinking about her cutting herself like that. And I can't stop thinking about that colossal argument that flared up in her house. The way Sylvia reacted, I'm pretty sure that it's a regular occurrence. Sylvia seemed to be handling it okay, the little I heard, but I can't help thinking that a kid shouldn't have to get involved in stuff like that. I mean, I've heard my mom and dad argue over things, and usually it's stuff that seems unimportant to me. But Madeleine and me, we don't interfere and it's blown over in a few minutes. There seemed real hatred in the shouting and yelling I heard coming from Sylvia's house. And I just can't get past the picture I have in my mind of that slob of a father of hers as a dirty brutal bully. I can't help worrying about Sylvia, I really can't. I wonder if he hits Sylvia. I'm wondering about that a lot, even though I know that I shouldn't.

When I reach my house, I see Mom's car in the driveway and next to it is Madeleine's little BMW coupe. If Dad's car is in the garage, then everyone is home.

I guess that everyone has gone to bed as I close the door behind me. The house is dark and quiet. I creep up the stairs with the lights off. It's not like I don't know where I'm going, after all. On the landing, I see a blue light flickering under Madeleine's door. She's watching TV. Or— more likely—she's fallen asleep watching

TV. We both have a habit of doing that. Like I think I've told you before, I've lost count of the number of times I've woken up to find some endlessly laughable shopping channel beaming at me.

My door clicks as I open it, and I'm about to step inside when Madeleine calls out to me as quietly as she can.

"Tom, is that you?"

I push her door open a little and pop my head inside.

"Sure it's me. Who were you expecting, Richard Ramirez?"

She ignores my wise-ass remark.

"Have you got a minute?"

"Sure."

I lie on the bed next to her. The room is dark except for the flickering light from the TV, and she's still dressed in jeans and a

T-shirt. This is very unlike her, so I know that she has something on her mind. Perhaps she's ready to talk to me about it now.

For a minute we just lie there while a rerun of *Seinfeld* plays out on the screen, but neither of us is in the mood to laugh.

"Tom…"

"Yeah?"

"I'm in trouble."

Next thing you know, she's crying and she's turned to me and her arms are around me so that all I can do is hold her and her face is buried in my shoulder and she's sobbing fit to break your heart. All I can do is stroke her hair and try to comfort her. There's no point saying anything because she's sobbing so much she can't listen. I have to let her get the worst of it out of her system. But I'm sick with worry now because I've never seen Madeleine like this. I realize that I'm not even worrying about Sylvia any more because Madeleine is right here and, well…

and well this is my Madeleine and she needs me to focus on her.

She can't sob with that kind of intensity forever and eventually it subsides. And we're just lying together and I'm still holding her and stroking her hair and old Seinfeld is still making sarcastic wisecracks with his dumb-ass friends on the TV.

"So come on then; tell me what's happened that's so bad."

She pulls herself away from me and she's looking at me. She's holding me with her eyes like Sylvia had done earlier and she's very serious.

"Oh Tom, I don't know what to do."

She starts to cry again so that I can see the sparkling tears run down her cheeks but she's not sobbing this time. I reach across to wipe the tears from her face with the back of my fingers.

"Hey, what can be so bad? It can't be

anything that money can't fix can it?"

I'm trying to make a joke, get her to lighten up a little so that she can open up and tell me what's going on. But really, it's not such a stupid thing to say. We certainly do have plenty of money and there are plenty of problems that money can fix. It's unfair, I know, but it's true. It really is. We can't help being the children of wealthy parents.

"Tom... I'm pregnant."

I'm not kidding; she just comes out and says it. Just like that. But what can I say? I mean, part of me is glad that it's just that and nothing worse. At least she's not in trouble with the law or anything. All the same, I'm numb with shock.

"Does Mom know?"

This is a really stupid question because I can tell that she hasn't told Mom, but I have to say something.

"Christ no! I can't tell her. I can't tell

anyone. I don't know what to do."

"You're going to have to tell her. You're going to need help, you're going to need someone..."

"I can't tell her! She thinks I'm going to college next year. It's all she ever talks about. She'll go crazy."

Well, actually, while I'm still in shock, I'm rational enough to know that Mom is unlikely to wig out over this. But I can imagine all the preaching that Madeleine is going to have to endure. Mom can make her disappointment last for a long, long time.

"Does David know? How does he feel about it?"

Yes, of course I'm assuming that David is the father; my sister is no cheap slut. And at this point I'm realizing that this is all too much to burden a sixteen year-old boy with, so I want someone else to be there for Madeleine. But when I look at her, the tears are running again.

"David won't talk to me. He won't even take my calls."

Well, David is a bastard. I can come to instant judgments like that. And more especially where my sister is concerned.

"But he has to take responsibility with you. He's in this with you."

I feel like going to his house right now and making a scene, I swear to God that I do.

"He said that he's too young to have his life ruined."

Well I know that David's family have big plans for him and everything—it's a burden that the children of wealthy families have to bear, as Madeleine and I know only too well. But just who does this asshole think he is? This is my sister!

This is a lot to throw on my plate and

I can feel myself growing up prematurely as the tears roll down Madeleine's cheeks. I know that I can't let my anger show because it just won't help her.

"Do you want to keep the baby?"

This is a harsh question to ask at this point, but I don't know what else to say.

"God no. I can't. Oh Tom, I can't, I can't."

She's holding me and sobbing again. So I let her sob it all away, until after a while she's calm again.

"Tom?"

"Yeah?"

"Will you come with me?

I'm suddenly cold because I know exactly what she's talking about.

"Come with you where?"

Like I don't know.

"To the clinic. Next Saturday."

"What clinic?"

"I'm going to have an abortion. It's all I can do, Tom. It will be best for everybody."

Well she's certainly made her mind up fast. I guess this is not like choosing a new pair of shoes, but I'm reeling all the same.

"Christ Maddie, are you sure that's what you want?"

"It's for the best, Tom. Trust me it's best for everyone. I want to make an appointment for next Saturday. Will you come with me Tom? Please say that you will. Please."

Well, in all my life I've never been able to say no to Madeleine and whatever I think, I'm not going to let her down now. Not that I care either way about the baby myself, you understand. As a matter of fact, babies leave me cold, they really do. They are all ugly, despite what their parents think, and beyond that they're just noise and stinking smells and responsibility. I guess if that point of view doesn't change, I'm not destined to make anything like a good father myself, but I don't care about that right now.

"What about Mom and Dad? Won't they want to know where we're going? It's going to be hard to hide that from them. You're not going to be yourself when we get back home, let's face it."

I'm not trying to change her mind; I just want to know that she's thought it through.

"That's why I want to have it done next Saturday."

She says it like she's talking about getting a pedicure.

"Mom and Dad are going to be away for the weekend. There's a weekend house party. They are going to be gone from Friday night through Sunday."

She really has been giving this some thought. I'm wondering just how long she's known that she's pregnant. And I can't help thinking of her having to go through all this on her own.

A wicked thought flits through my mind about the party that Mom and Dad are going to. They do this from time to time and I have my suspicions concerning just what kind of party this might be. You probably already realize that I suspect it to be a swingers' party. The thought of them satisfying their degenerate lust while their daughter is breaking herself up just sickens me. It really does. And I realize that this makes me sound like some prudish moral zealot—which really I'm not—but it just doesn't seem right that they are going to be acting like Roman aristocracy while their children are hurting. This is wrong, of course, because they'll never know what we are going through and I imagine that they would be there for us if they did. All the same, it's how I feel.

"Have you made an appointment already?"

I'm just wondering because this is the first I've heard about this party that Mom and Dad are apparently going to.

"No. I'm going to call on Monday to make the arrangements. You will come with me, won't you?"

Like I said, I'm not in the habit of refusing Madeleine anything. I'm not going to change that now.

"Of course I will. You know I will."

I sit with Madeleine until she drifts off to sleep. I don't know what time it is when I go back to my own room, but when I slide into bed, I realize that I haven't been thinking of Sylvia at all. Why can't life be simple?

CHAPTER 11

My funny valentine

It's nine-thirty when I wake up. This is very late for me, but let's face it, I was late getting to sleep.

I take a long, hot shower and it's so soothing that I find it difficult to switch off the jets and finish it. But of course I do, and I wrap a towel around myself and saunter back to my room, yawning.

I notice that Madeleine's door is closed and I hope that she is sleeping. All that sobbing will have tired her out. I'm still concerned for Madeleine, of course, but today I am going to visit Sylvia. So I'm thinking of Sylvia as I dress. Sylvia, Sylvia,

Sylvia. As if I don't have enough to worry about with Madeleine and all. When I think of Sylvia, all I can think of is that massive argument that she walked right into in her house last night. That sure as hell did sound violent. So now I'm just wondering if Sylvia is okay. I wonder if I should call Sylvia to see if she still wants me to come around this afternoon, but I think better of it. She just might have changed her mind after what happened last night. And sure, I realize that that makes me sound incredibly insecure. And maybe I am. But I'm not going to risk it all the same. I'm just going to show up at her place and present her with a *fait accompli*. Isn't that what you would do?

So I'm sitting downstairs with the TV on and not really watching anything. Well actually, I'm watching the clock, if I'm really honest. And have you noticed that when you're waiting for something that you're looking forward to, how time just stands still? It does. It really does.

And I keep trying to think of things to do to occupy me while I wait, but a kind of lethargy has set in. It's like all I want to do is focus on the clock. And the fact that it isn't moving.

Apart from the TV, the house is quiet. Mom and Dad are out—they've gone shopping for something or other that they can't possibly need—and I haven't seen a sign of Madeleine. Sometimes I get up and wander around the living room and look out of the window, as if that is going to help the time move faster. I'm focused on Sylvia so much that it must be the twentieth time I've looked out of that big old window before I realize that Madeleine's car is not in the driveway next to Mom's. Wow, I wonder what time Madeleine got up and went out. I sure as hell never heard her. Well, I won't be able to ask her if I can borrow some nail polish and stuff to take over to Sylvia's. I'll just have to assume that it's okay—which I'm sure it is. Madeleine won't mind.

At last the clock has moved some. I'm walking down Sylvia's street. People are washing cars in the driveways, cutting the grass in front of their houses. All typical suburban stuff, I guess, but it's all a lot noisier than where I live. Now and then you can hear a dog barking and little kids are playing—in backyards I suppose because I can't see any out on the street.

As I near Sylvia's house, I'm strangely nervous. I guess I'm wondering if there will be an atmosphere. That sure sounded like a fierce fight last night. And I still have this picture of her dad as a slob in a dirty vest and I can't get past how aggressive he's sounded on the couple of times I've called Sylvia's house. I'm telling myself that I must be wrong, because the people I'm seeing on this street are nice and clean and wonderfully suburban, and the cars in the driveways are all pretty new and well-maintained. But the image persists all the same.

For some reason, standing outside Sylvia's front door, I can hardly believe that I have pushed the button to ring the bell. But I must have, because the door is opening and then there is Sylvia and she's smiling and I can just smell the soap and the scent and stuff. She's wearing jeans and a strappy pink top and no shoes and she looks just absolutely gorgeous.

"Well, are you going to come in?"

The house is pretty quiet as Sylvia closes the door behind me. It's smaller than our place, for sure, but it's neat and it's light and not at all like I was expecting. You know, I'd actually built up this stupid picture in my head of the house being a bit dingy and perhaps a little run-down. And where do you suppose I got this idea from? Well I know that it came from the image I have of Sylvia's dad, and that's only based on the few words I've heard him bellow on the phone. Anyway, the point is that images we create in our heads can be way off the mark.

We're standing in a small entrance hall and off to the left is the kitchen, and a guy is stepping out. He's kind of tall and well groomed and he's dressed in tan cotton Dockers and a polo shirt with the unmistakable Ralph Lauren logo on the chest. It's like looking in a mirror in a way, because I'm wearing tan Dockers and a Ralph Lauren shirt too, although mine is green and his is lilac. Of course, I'm not a hundred years old like this guy, but that's some coincidence, wouldn't you say?

"Snap!"

It's a second or two before I realize that the guy is talking to me. I see Sylvia rolling her eyes to the ceiling.

"Just ignore him. This is my dad and he'd do just about anything to embarrass me.'

The guy is grinning, and despite the words I can tell that Sylvia and he are quite close. It's just banter, and I recognize it because it's how me and my mom are together. You've seen that for yourself. And remember what I was just saying, about images in our heads being way off the mark? Well, if this is Sylvia's dad, then I have been totally wrong. No dirty vest stretching over a paunch. No lack of grooming. No lack of humor either. You know, it's *so* hard to match the guy standing before me with my telephone experience of him that it makes me wonder if I'd been calling the wrong house! But of course I hadn't been, because Sylvia came to the phone. And actually, it's something of a relief to find that he's not the slob of my imagination, if you want to know the truth. That's an image I can throw out with the trash, thank God.

"So aren't you going to tell me who this is?"

Sylvia looks at her dad and rolls her eyes again. I'm seeing that Sylvia can be very theatrical.

"Dad, this is Tom. He goes to my school and he's in my year, but we're not in the same classes. Is that okay or do you want to interrogate him?"

Her dad ignores this sarcasm. He's looking at me. At least Sylvia hasn't said that my name is Holden, so that's something, I guess.

"Tom eh? I'll try to remember that. Another one to add to the list."

By the time he's finished saying this he's already turned and he's disappeared into the living room. Sylvia's grabbed my hand and she's pulling me up the stairs. All I can hear is the muffled thump of her bare feet on the stair carpet but inside I'm cold as hell. Another one. That's what her dad had said. It's what he'd said on the phone that time too. I'm feeling sick inside. I really am. And I know that I shouldn't and that Sylvia and me have only just started seeing each other and everything. But I do believe that I'm jealous. I really do. And I don't even know what I'm jealous of. Or even if there's any need to be jealous at all. I'm just screwed up is what it is. I really am.

Anyway, Sylvia's room is not how I'd expected it to be. I'd been expecting dark walls, gothic posters of indie bands and stuff, and candles, but it isn't like that at all. The walls are pale pink and while there *are* posters, they are Sheryl Crow and Blondie and George Clooney—but *not* Tom

Cruise. And amazingly, the posters she's chosen do have color schemes that go with her walls. I'm impressed, I really am. The bed is quite big for the room, but it doesn't dominate, and there's a dressing table and a built-in wardrobe, all of stripped pine to match the bed. And there is surprisingly little clutter. Seriously, this is something I'd never expected, and you have to know that it delights me. I was expecting loads of stuffed toys and trash like that. But there are two bowls of colored glass beads on the dresser and a glass box that contains costume jewelry and stuff, and photographs of her mom and dad in a frame, and that's about it. I feel truly comfortable in this room.

I'm actually sitting at the foot of the bed, leaning back on it. Sylvia is sitting on the bed behind me and her legs are dangling over my shoulders. She has the prettiest little feet with perfect straight toes, but they're looking a little bit silly at the moment because of the foam toe-separators that are there to stop the nail polish from smudging while it dries. I've already done her fingers and now I'm doing her toes to match. I'm using the *I'm Not Really A Waitress* polish from the OPI Hollywood Collection. It's a really confident, rich red color that I feel suits Sylvia particularly well. Madeleine has been using it a lot lately and I took it from her dresser, but I'm sure she won't mind. If she ever even notices.

Looking up at the dressing table mirror in front of me I can see Sylvia inspecting her fingernails, holding her hands away from her and splaying the fingers out.

"You're really good. Do you know that? Salon good. I'm impressed."

Well I don't exactly glow with pride at that, because I *know* that I'm good. But hey, everyone enjoys compliments, right?

"Sure I know I'm good. I've had years of training at the hands of the most demanding client."

"Your sister, right?"

"Yeah, my sister."

She's made me think of Madeleine and I wonder where Madeleine is right now. I can't stop thinking of her sobbing if you really want to know, and that just about kills me.

We're just sitting here, waiting for the polish to dry, and listening to—this came as a major surprise, trust me—Chet Baker playing mellow jazz, when I notice a small pair of nail scissors on the dresser, next to one of the bowls of glass beads. I can just about reach them as I lean forward, so I pick them up. They are chrome and sharp and pointed.

Actually, the music is kind of hypnotic and we're not talking much as we listen to it so I don't really imagine that Sylvia has even noticed that I've picked the scissors up. Truth is, the music has a slightly melancholic air to it, and I get to thinking about her dad describing me as *another one*, and who the *others* might be and what they might mean to Sylvia. And I'm on the verge of making myself stupid and silly about it.

"What the hell do you think you're doing?"

Sylvia seems angry and I can't imagine what she's talking about. And then I notice what I *am* doing. I have the scissors in one hand, and I've opened them out. And without even realizing I'm doing it, I'm running the sharp point up along the inside of my forearm. I'm pressing hard, but not quite hard enough to break the skin. All the same, I'm leaving deep red marks. And I realize that these marks sort of mirror the scars on Sylvia's arm.

"Do you think that's funny? Or are you just dumb-ass crazy or something?"

Before I can answer, she's swinging her legs over my head and she's getting up off the bed. She's having to walk back on her heels like a duck because of the toe-separators but I'm not laughing, or even smiling. Sylvia is crazy upset, and I didn't even realize what I was doing. I never meant to upset her, and that's the certain truth.

She snatches the scissors out of my hand

and she's holding one of the points against the scars on her own arm. She's glaring at me and I don't know what to say, so I say nothing. Then I see her soften and she just throws those scissors across the room. I don't see where they fall—I just hear them hit a wall—because I'm fixed on her. She's looking over my head, not looking at me.

"I'm sorry. I guess I know you didn't mean anything by it."

"I didn't even know I was doing it. I swear to God I didn't."

She sits on the bed next to where I'm still sitting on the floor. We are talking to each other's reflection in the dresser mirror, like we are too fragile to face up to our words directly.

"I know. I know you didn't."

"So what's the matter?"

"I'm not ashamed of these scars on my arm you know. But I'm not proud of them either. And I just kind of freaked out, seeing you running those scissors against your skin. I don't know. I guess I really thought you were going to do it."

"Really? Wow, I wasn't even thinking of it. I don't think I'd have the nerve, to tell you the truth."

Actually, I'd been pressing that scissor point in pretty damn hard if you must know. To the point where it was hurting, but only just enough so that it was almost becoming a pleasure. I know, I know that sounds sick and unbelievable, but I can only tell you, that's exactly how it felt. And I'm going to confess to you here, I had been wondering—just wondering—what it would be like to simply press the point a little harder; to break the skin and watch the rivulets of blood run down my arm. To stare at them until all I could do was watch, until I just lost myself in seeing red. You can see why I don't say any of this to Sylvia though, right?

Sylvia is taking me at face value. And she suddenly turns round on her knees so that she's facing me. I find myself hoping that she's not smudging that polish on her toes—I'd done a fantastic job, I swear to God—but that thought quickly passes because Sylvia is smiling a sultry smile that seems experienced way beyond her sixteen years.

"I'm glad to hear that, Tom. Because there sure are better ways of passing the time."

Before you know it, we are wrapped around each other and it's just like a continuation of that kiss from last night on the doorstep. She really gives herself to the kiss, so that all you can do is let go with her. Which I do. And the last thing I can honestly tell you is that through it all, I can hear old Chet Baker mumbling something about a funny valentine or something, and that it seems just about appropriate. I could tell you more, but I'm not going to. Figure it out for yourself.

CHAPTER 12

A weight off my mind

It's been a strange sort of week so far. From the outside, you could look at it and think that it's been pretty tedious and dull and ordinary for me. I get up in the morning, I choose what I'm going to wear, I go to school, I come home again. But it hasn't felt ordinary. I feel like I've been existing in a fog.

Take school for example. It sounds pretty nerdish to say it, I know, but most of the time I don't mind school. Sometimes I quite enjoy it. I'm quite academic really, and I guess that most of it comes easy to me. But this week I haven't been interested. When I'm there, all I'm thinking about is

Sylvia. And I'm always just looking out for her. I swear to God, all I do is think about her and I'm moping around at break times trying to see if I can find her. And I know how stupid and dangerous that is, because I'm pretty certain that she doesn't spend all her time thinking about me, and it's pretty obvious that she doesn't make any effort to seek *me* out. Don't get me wrong, she always seems happy enough when I do find her, and she's happy to pass the time with me. She's not distant or anything like that. In fact, she's quite affectionate really. Thing is, there's been a couple of days this week when she hasn't showed up for school at all and although I know I'm being stupid, I'm tearing myself up wondering where she is and what she's doing when she isn't there. That is stupid isn't it? Yeah, I know it is.

I'm also looking out for Eddie all the time. Although actually, Eddie caught me unawares just this morning, by the lockers. And he was okay with me, as it happens. I mean, he wasn't like the Eddie who had been my best friend or anything, but he didn't try to beat me into the ground or anything and there was no mention of me being a perv or anything. In fact, he even spoke to me.

"I hear you've been seeing Sylvia Reynolds. Is that right?"

I'm stunned to hear him speak to me at all.

"Er, yeah. I have. I've just seen her a couple of times. Nothing serious."

Have I told you before how casually and effectively I'm able to lie? Eddie just nods like he's the sage of romance or something.

"I saw her out on the town last night. She's cute. I guess we can say for sure now that you're not gay."

And Eddie just slams his locker shut and turns and walks away.

So Sylvia was out on the town last night. And she's not at to school today. Well you can imagine the thoughts racing through my mind. What was she doing, where was she going? Who was she with? Yeah, that's the question all right. That's the one it all boils down to. Who was she with?

Of course I just want to run after Eddie and ask him this very question, but I don't. I don't want Eddie to know just how stuck I am on Sylvia. I don't want anyone to know. And worse, I'm scared of what the answer might be. Because all I can see are visions of Sylvia out on the town with someone else, laughing that laugh of hers and having a great time and it's killing me. Do you get that? It's killing me, it's choking me up inside.

So I'm sitting on my bed and I'm chewing this over again and again and again; round and round it goes, the same cycle of thoughts, and I don't feel any better for it.

And every time I see Madeleine I feel the burden of the secret that she's shared with me. We've barely spoken to each other all week and it's Thursday night now. It's nearly Saturday. And we know what's going to happen on Saturday.

So there it is; I'm carrying Madeleine's secret like I'm carrying her unborn child, because that's how heavy and scary it feels to me. And Mom thinks that I'm a feeble victim and wants me to change schools. And I'm stressing about Sylvia to the point where all I can see is the city at night and people and bars, and there she is with some guy. He looks cool and older than me, so I guess that I'm basing his image on Madeleine's bastard boyfriend David. Everyone is having a good time and Sylvia is laughing at his jokes and putting her hand up to her mouth like she does, and sometimes they're sharing intimate talk and she just touches his arm so that it makes me sick inside to see it. And they're dancing. And then they're slow-dancing and they're holding each other. And then her lips are pressing against his so that I can actually feel them against goddamn mine.

So you're wondering how the scissors came to be in my hand? Well I can't tell you. They're from a cabinet in the bathroom and I can't even remember *going* to the bathroom. All I know is that I'm sitting at the foot of my bed like I sat at the foot of Sylvia's bed. I went out and bought a goddamn Chet Baker CD and that's so depressing it might as well be Leonard Cohen or Nick Cave, and the only light is the flicker from the goddamn TV which is playing with the sound turned down.

I can see the scissors all right though. I've been tracing stripes up and down my forearm with one of the points. For some while now, I guess, because I can see the pink tracks where I've been pressing it into the skin. Now I'm just staring at one of the points where it's digging in to my flesh. I can't feel anything. I just see it. I'm detached from what I'm looking at, like it's someone else's arm. Sylvia's arm, maybe. And I push the point harder and I still feel nothing, but there's a deep indentation now. And I push some more and then I feel a tiny sting, and I can see that I've burst the skin because a little blob of blood is building up around the point. But that's all there is. This tiny sting and then nothing. I'm still watching, like I'm in a trance or something. The point is still dug in there, beneath the skin, and the blob of blood has started to run. I don't feel it, and as I look I don't even see the arm as my arm at all. It's Sylvia's arm. And it's fascinating to watch as I draw the scissor point up my arm and more blood follows this track. It hurts at first, but Sylvia is right; only for a moment. I'm watching the blood flow and I feel that it's my blood and Sylvia's blood, like this act is bonding us somehow. And more rivulets are running over and around my arm. They're dripping onto my legs but I don't feel that at all. Everything else that was weighing down on me has gone. I'm just watching. Until all I'm doing is just seeing red.

CHAPTER 13

I can't be responsible

Well, it's Friday morning and I'm standing in the bathroom. I'm standing in front of the mirror, but I'm not looking at myself like I normally would. I'm checking the tight bandages around my arm. You can see a ragged red track on the outside of the gauze where the blood has seeped through. I cut myself pretty damn deep last night. It didn't hurt then though, and it doesn't hurt now. Sylvia was right about that. All the same, I feel bad about myself for having done it. I wonder if I'll have a scar like one of Sylvia's. Do I really want that?

There's a knock at the bathroom door.

"Tom, are you in there?"

It's Madeleine. The knock is subdued and so is her voice. Of course, I know just why that is and you do too. But do you know what bugs me? Makes me feel angry if you really want to know? Poor old Madeleine has been like this all week. She's been withdrawn and quiet, and that is so unlike her. And Mom and Dad haven't even noticed. Can you believe that? Goddamn, they haven't even noticed and it's their own daughter and she's obviously in trouble or something and they haven't even said a word. I guess that they're drooling over the sordid weekend party they're planning to go to, the goddamn deviants.

Yeah yeah, I know that they love us and everything, but would it be too much to ask that they take an interest in us? Seems that way. Right now, I just hate Mom and Dad. I really do.

So I slip on my Dior robe and I'm truly thankful that it has long sleeves that are a little too big for me really, and I open the door. Madeleine is standing outside and she's wearing a big fluffy terry robe that looks like it's wrapping her in giant soft folds. It looks just like it's comforting her if you want to know, and I wonder if that's why Madeleine is wearing it. It's no substitute for Mom, who should be comforting her, though. Goddamn Mom.

"You okay Maddie?"

I'm kind of concerned because she doesn't look okay at all. She looks like she just wants to cry, and if I tell you the truth, seeing her like that makes *me* want to cry along with her.

"Yeah, Tom. I'm okay."

It's obvious that she's not, but I'm not going to push it. She looks very tired, is how she looks. And maybe she *has* been crying. It's hard to say.

"Well, you take care of yourself today Maddie. I'll stay away from school if you want me to."

"No. No, Tom. You go to school. I'm okay, honest."

She isn't fooling herself and she isn't fooling me. I'm not going to push it though. Fact is, even though I *would* have stayed home to be with Madeleine, I'm really desperate to get to school today. I'm tearing myself up wanting to see Sylvia. I still can't get over her being out on the town the other night and not being in school yesterday. I'm feeling totally sick with the thoughts racing through my head and I know I'm stupid and jealous but I just can't fight it. I hate myself for that, but I don't know what to do to make these thoughts go away. I really don't. So I have to go to school just to see Sylvia, even though *that* starts me wondering if she'll even show up today, and *that* makes me feel even worse. If that's at all possible. I'm screwed up. I know it.

Out on the landing there, I just put an arm around Madeleine and kiss her softly on the cheek. I hear the bathroom door close behind me as I wander back to my room. Poor Madeleine.

At school, I'm dressed in a jacket and a long sleeved shirt, for obvious reasons, even though it *is* a scorching hot day. The bell has rung and the kids are all making their way over to the main doors. I'm hanging around as long as I can, hoping to see Sylvia arrive. It doesn't look like she's coming in again. My head feels like a swarm of wasps as I turn to follow the last few stragglers. Even my cut arm is beginning to sting and ache.

I have geography and French this morning, but while I'm sitting in the classroom I'm not listening to a goddamn word. Somehow I get away with it. I'm just staring out of the windows and wishing that I were dead. I mean that. I feel sick and tired and sorry for myself and I just think it would be better if I was dead. I'm not saying that I feel suicidal. I'm just saying that I hate the way I feel and I hate my life, and I just wish that things were the way they were a few weeks ago. Actually, that's not quite true. What I'm *really* wishing is that things could be back like they were but I still had Sylvia. Not asking much, huh?

Well, at morning break I'm sitting alone under a tree and I'm staring at the school gates. It's like I'm hoping that Sylvia will walk through them, that she's just late or something. I'd usually be reading a book, but this morning I'm not. I'm just staring and wallowing in my stupid self-pitying thoughts.

"Hey Holden. What are you up to, sitting out here all alone?"

The voice is coming from behind me and you know who it is just as well as I do. Besides, who else ever calls me Holden?

She's sitting down beside me even as I turn to look at her, and she's wearing this amazing cotton-print summer dress with large geometric shapes in bright primary colors. I'm so pleased to see her that I almost think I'm going to be sick.

"I was looking for you yesterday."

Now I know that that makes me sound like a needy jerk, even as I'm saying it, but

I just can't stop myself. What I'm really saying is that I want her to tell me where she was. And who she was with. In other words, I'm prying and I hate myself for it. She's not falling for it though.

"Oh, I just didn't feel like coming in. Hey, you did a great job with my nails."

She's just changing the subject and even I can see that, plain as day. She's wiggling her toes and flapping her fingers in front of me and I can see that the polish hasn't chipped even though it's been a few days. But to tell the truth, I'm not even interested. Just what is it that she's goddamn keeping from me? It's all I can do not to come straight out and ask her. Only God knows where I find the strength not to.

"Yeah, I told you I was good."

Pretty feeble I know, but a million times better than what I want to say. Then I notice her face. It's a little swollen and red beneath her left eye. It looks like someone has hit her. It goddamn really looks like someone has hit her. It's not as livid as it could be, so it's probably a day or so old now.

"What happened to your face?"

I suppose that I shouldn't have asked, but the words are out there now and I can't take them back.

She turns her face away.

"Oh nothing. I tripped in the living room and hit my face on the coffee table. How stupid is that? You should have seen it yesterday. That's why I didn't come in."

Well come on. I'm not dumb. I know that's a lie. She knows that's a lie. And she knows that I know that that's a lie. But how can I push it? Truth is, I'm so goddamn scared of alienating her that I can't say anything. Does that make me a coward? I sure as hell think that it does.

"When did it happen?"

As if that matters.

"Wednesday night. I feel like an idiot."

Wednesday night. The night that Eddie saw her out on the town. A million and one thoughts are flashing through my head now. She was with a guy and he hit her, the bastard. She came in late and... Oh my God, that's it. Her *dad* hit her. The goddamn lousy cowardly slob. *He* hit her. And I bet he's hit her before. Oh the cowardly dirty trash. It *must* be him. He has a temper. He's very aggressive. I've heard him. I know it's him!

Well of course, I don't *know* anything of the kind. But I've made up my mind. Her dad beats her up. But I can't say any of this. What *can* I say?

"Should I kiss it better?"

That's feeble again, but like I said, I can't blurt out what I'm thinking.

She smiles, that dirty, sultry, sexy smile of hers, and she leans towards me.

"Mmm… the *kiss* part sounds good…"

She puts her hand on my arm to steady herself and then she pulls away and her hand is gently feeling the bandage beneath my shirt.

"Hey, what's happened to you?"

"Nothing. Just a cut."

I'm so drained that I can't even think of a decent lie. She's unbuttoning my shirt and rolling up the sleeve and I just sit there and let her. Pretty soon she's looking at the bandage and the blood stain and all, and she seems pretty shocked.

"Christ, what have you done?"

She's looking at me like I'm an alien or something and I don't like that look on her face one little bit. She's leaning back away from me now, like she's just heard that I've got an infectious disease.

"It's nothing. It's just a cut. It'll heal."

I'm trying to act all cool but I'm actually shaking and I'm hoping like hell that she doesn't notice.

"You've done this to yourself haven't you?"

I can't answer.

"Christ Tom, you stupid, stupid jerk."

I liked it better when she was calling me Holden.

"This is because of me, isn't it? I just knew it. I knew it the other day when I saw how you were playing with those scissors. Christ."

"It's nothing, really."

I want her to believe that. I want to believe it myself but the truth is, she's right.

"I think we should stop seeing each other, before this goes further."

"No..."

I'm really shaking now, so that I feel like I couldn't get up even if I tried. I can feel the blood rushing to my face even as I feel cold inside.

"You don't have to do something just because I've done it."

"I know. I…"

"I can't be responsible for this, Tom. I just can't. It's best that we end this right now. I can't handle this. It's too much."

I don't exactly sit there as she gets up and starts to walk back inside but I'm struggling to get to my feet because I'm shaking so much and I feel really weak.

"Sylvia…"

She doesn't even turn to look back at me. And pretty soon, I can't even see her. My eyes are full of tears, I don't mind admitting it. I'm just crying fit to break your heart, if you must know, and leaning against that goddamn tree.

CHAPTER 14

Making allowances

Well Chet goddamn Baker is playing again and my room is dark, with not even the flicker of the TV tonight. The whole house seems under some sort of black cloud. There's only Madeleine and me at home; Mom and Dad are away at their goddamn orgy or whatever it is, and I'm scared.

I'm scared of how I feel right now, and I'm scared about tomorrow. I hate Sylvia for walking away from me like she did, even though I realize that I actually love her. I hate the fact that Madeleine is going to be depending on me because I don't feel strong enough, I just don't. And I hate Mom and

Dad for not being here. And I hate myself for being weak and being scared.

Of course I'm holding the scissors again. The dirty, blood-soiled bandage is on the floor next to me. In places the cut from last night is still weeping blood and plasma, but it's not really flowing. And I'm just playing at these open wounds with the tip of the scissors and I'm feeling nothing. I'm just numb with fear.

Madeleine is downstairs watching TV. At least she was when I last saw her. She's watching a DVD—a recording of some ghastly stage musical that we'd all been to see last year. Normally, I'd tease her for that. I mean, musical theater is surely the lowest, meanest, least intelligent art form imaginable isn't it? I'd rather watch rats mating than sit through a minute of that drivel. It's like baby food for the minds of morons; all sickly mush is what it is. I have to make allowances for Madeleine right now though. She has other things to consider and I know it.

When I walked past Madeleine's room earlier, I saw her little overnight bag on her bed. I've never seen anything so lonely and sad in my entire life as that bag just sitting there. Madeleine has packed a change of clothes for tomorrow. It's not like she is going to stay overnight or anything; she just wants something fresh to put on once it's all done and finished.

I'm sitting here trying to put myself in Madeleine's shoes, to feel what she's feeling, but I'm so wrapped up in my own misery and self-pity that I can't. I despise myself for that. Madeleine needs me more than ever right now and I'm just useless. Perhaps I've always been useless. Selfish and useless. What use am I to anyone? Sylvia's getting beaten up and I can't do anything. Madeleine is hurting and there's only me to help her and all I'm concerned with is my own depression.

I can feel the blood running over my arm again. I'd better get another bandage. I should really go and sit with my sister. Did I ever tell you how much I love her? It might not seem like it, the way I'm acting right now, but the truth is that I do. I really do. I love her to bits if you must know.

CHAPTER 15

Mondrian, Kandinsky and Rive Gauche in the clinic

Madeleine is driving. It's early Saturday morning so there isn't a lot of traffic. We've had to drive through the city, because that's the quickest way to get to the clinic. Normally, we'd be singing. We'd have the iPod hooked up and we'd be singing along and laughing while the world rushed by outside. But today all we have for company is the engine noise, and the sound of the tires as they swoosh across the asphalt. It's a sunny day outside and scorching hot, but we don't even have the top down. I'm not even wearing shades.

The clinic is deep in the countryside, way beyond the city. It takes an hour to drive there, and Madeleine pulls her little BMW in through the discreet gates. The wheels crunch on the gravel of the driveway. I can feel Madeleine's tension as she sits beside me and I know that she's scared. I'm just hoping and praying that she can't tell that I'm scared too. I just have to be strong for her.

I'm carrying Madeleine's cute little overnight bag and I follow her into the sterile white building. The reception area is actually quite light and the walls are painted pastel shades and there are prints on the walls—Mondrian and Kandinsky. And there are low padded couches upholstered in soft fabrics, and glass-topped tables strewn with magazines.

I don't pay attention as Madeleine speaks to the woman sitting behind the reception desk, but pretty soon she's asking me for her bag, and before I know it, I'm just standing there looking at her as she's led by a nurse through a set of doors. She doesn't even turn to look back, and the feeling I get is that I'm watching her being led off to a prison cell on death row.

I must look the way I feel, too, because that receptionist—who is wearing Rive Gauche perfume—is right beside me and she's holding my arm very gently. I'm letting her lead me to one of the couches. I notice the receptionist now like it's the first time I've seen her. She must be in her thirties and she's wearing a white smock that suits her and sort of just hints at her curves so that I find myself thinking that it's actually very sexy on her. On her finger there is a thick gold wedding band and a ring with a diamond that's so big that I'm wondering if perhaps she's married to a doctor. She's smiling at me and offering to get me a drink and just being so kind that I just hope that her husband makes her happy. She's just the sort of person who deserves to be always happy. I want to cry because she is so kind and I can sense that she would be sympathetic, but that would not be fair on her, so I hold it back. Even so, she sits down next to me and she's close and I'm so upset that I'm almost intoxicated by her lovely perfume.

"Your sister's very lucky to have a brother like you."

I look up at her and her smile is so gentle and soft that I can't help myself. The tears start to flow and I'm sobbing and she's holding me. And I'm not just crying for Madeleine; I'm crying for Sylvia too, and I'm crying for myself because all of a sudden I don't feel strong. And while the receptionist holds me and strokes my hair I continue to cry because I want my mom. Mom should be here for us. It's Mom's job to look after us, is what I'm thinking.

"She'll be fine, don't worry."

The receptionist is still letting me cry all over her and stroking my hair. I feel like I could stay like this forever.

Of course I don't though. And now it's a few hours later and I'm still sitting on that couch when the swing doors open and Madeleine is being wheeled into the reception area on a chrome-framed chair. Madeleine looks drained and pale and old in that chair so that I almost lose it again. I even feel the tears well up in my eyes, but seeing Madeleine gives me strength. I can control myself for her sake. I think the receptionist notices though. She is looking at me, and she nods gently and smiles. She even winks at me, like she's saying that everything has turned out okay, just like she'd told me it would.

I want to know what Madeleine is feeling right now, but she doesn't seem to want to talk. She seems like a zombie, really. I just want to get her home.

So we're driving through the city again. It's mid-afternoon now, and there is plenty of traffic. Lots of people on the streets, too. I'm behind the wheel of course, even though I don't have a license. It's a risk we've taken many times before and actually, I'm a really excellent driver.

Madeleine hasn't said more than a word. She's looking at the dashboard and her arms are folded loosely across her tummy, like she has mild indigestion or something. I don't really want to think about what she's just been through. I just want to get her home where I can take care of her.

We don't have any music on again, so I'm glancing at the people walking on the streets. Heading for the stores, I'm guessing. And it's while I'm scanning the people and wishing that Madeleine and me could swap places with two of them, that I nearly crash the car. It's true, I nearly swerve into another car and Madeleine has to grab the wheel momentarily.

"Christ, Tom!"

She doesn't have to say more than that. And I feel deep shame at letting her down like that as I carry on through the traffic and towards home. So I guess you're wondering what I must have seen to make me lose control like that. Well I'll tell you. I saw Sylvia. Walking down the street in a black lace-trimmed summer dress and sandals and sunglasses, and she looked happy, like there was nothing on earth that could possibly matter on such a perfect day as this. And she was with a guy and they were holding hands. I could still make out the shade of polish that I'd painted on her nails. Yeah, they were holding hands. Right up to the moment when they stopped and turned to each other and she was standing on her toes to kiss him.

You can see now why I nearly crashed the car, right? I feel sick. I really do want to be sick. It's tight up in my throat and my head is everywhere. I just want to be home. Christ, I need to be home.

CHAPTER 16

I want my mom

It's a quiet Sunday. I stayed in with Madeleine yesterday after we got back, but I don't know how much of a comfort I was to her. She had severe stomach cramps— as you'd expect—so I laid her on the couch and sat on the floor next to her while we watched TV. I can't even tell you what we watched, to be honest. Because all the time, I could only think of Sylvia.

I'm thinking of Sylvia now. I'm in Madeleine's room, and guess what? We're watching TV, even though it's only mid-morning. Madeleine seems to be in a lot of pain, judging from the occasional grimaces and groans. I've asked her if she wants to go to the hospital, but she says that the pain will pass and that she just needs time. I can't argue with that—what would I know? But I do know Madeleine, and I can tell that it's not the physical pain that hurts her the most. So I just stroke her feet, which I know she likes, and my mind comes back time and time again to Sylvia.

I've called Sylvia's house, of course. Enough times to be classed as a stalker, to be honest. And needless to say, I've not managed to speak to Sylvia; just had the occasional terse exchange with her father. Funny, I'm not even thinking about how much I hate him as I speak to him. I'm not thinking about how aggressive and unhelpful he is, and I'm not even thinking about how he hits Sylvia. Rather selfishly, all I can think about is that I have no way of getting in touch with Sylvia short of going to her house. And there is no guarantee that she would be there. And what if she was, but that guy was with her? Would that make me feel better? I think we know the answer to that. Anyway, I can't leave Madeleine. Before there was Sylvia, there was always Madeleine. And no matter what happens, there always will be Madeleine. Why the hell can't Sylvia carry a cell phone? I hate her for that.

And now I can hear a car pulling into our driveway outside. Mom and Dad are back, obviously. Yesterday, I really wanted Mom to be around for us, but right now I'm not so sure. I'm being selfish, but the thing is, she's going to find out that Madeleine is unwell—we're obviously not going to tell her why—and she'll be fussing over Madeleine, just like she should, I guess. And that means that I'll be pushed to one side. And all I'll do then is churn over how I've seen Sylvia kissing that guy. God, I can feel Sylvia's kisses now and it brings a lump to my throat. I just want to die, thinking of Sylvia with that guy.

"Hi, we're home."

Mom has popped her head around the door. She is smiling her sweet smile at first, but that's quickly dropped and we're seeing her concerned Mom face now. Well you'd be concerned if you saw us, I guess. Madeleine suffering from stomach cramps and depression, and me just going quietly nuts. Yes, I am, really. I'm losing control. Sylvia is consuming me and I can't do anything about it. And now I'm going to have to be alone with my thoughts. I'm not sure that I can handle that.

But I do handle it, after a fashion. Mom has made Madeleine come downstairs and lie on the couch. Mom thinks that Madeleine is having severe period cramps, even though the timing would suggest that that would be unlikely. As if Mom would know that though. Mom is fussing over Madeleine and talking to her in a low voice, like they're sharing "secrets of the sisterhood." If I wasn't so miserably mired in my own self-pity I would sneer in contempt. What with the gazillion health lessons we've had at school over the years, and with having a sister as uninhibited as Madeleine, I reckon I know enough about the menstrual cycle to be a top-notch gynecologist. Still, I leave them to it.

It's night again, and I'm alone in my room. Last time I checked, Madeleine was looking a little perkier. Having Mom around to look after her has been a tonic after all. I am ashamed that I am so wrapped up in my own business that I haven't been a real brother to Madeleine at just the moment when she needed me most. I'll have to make it up to her some way, someday. Someday soon. But right now I just want to talk to Sylvia, so I pick up my phone and hit the number—yes, she's on my speed-dial list now.

The phone rings half a dozen times.

"Yeah, who is it?"

Sylvia's father, of course, but he doesn't sound quite as aggressive as he usually does.

"Is Sylvia there please?"

There's a pause and I'm waiting for the customary growl telling me that she's not available.

"Sylvia! Phone!"

Oh God. She's there. Now I feel nauseous and my chest tightens up. I was so expecting her not to be there that now she is, a tiny part of me is actually afraid.

"Hello?"

"Hi. It's only me."

I'm cringing at how my voice is squeaking. Surely she can feel my fear and lack of confidence. And surely she'll understand straight away the subtext to this call.

"Oh. Hi."

"I was just calling, you know, to see how you were."

"You shouldn't call. We shouldn't see each other Tom. I can't be responsible if you do something stupid. I can't afford to blame myself."

"But I'm not going to do anything stupid..."

I know, I know. I know how it looks. I've already *done* something stupid, so why should she believe me? Of course, she doesn't believe me, so that's okay then.

"Tom, I've got to go. You've got to stop calling."

I've been expecting that this call wouldn't go well, but short of stabbing me in the heart with an ice-cold dagger, I can't imagine how much worse it could be than just hearing her say those cruel words like that.

"But, honest—Sylvia…"

There's no point me continuing because she's hung up the phone. And I'm picturing her going back to her room and that guy being there. Bet you can imagine just how that feels, right? And I'm thinking of Madeleine downstairs and how she had been depending on me, and all I'd done was the least that I could do. And I'm sorry for myself because there's nobody here to look after me. And I'm hurting too. I want my mom. I really want my mom.

And now you can see that I'm crying. I'm silent because I don't want anyone to know, but you can see the tears as they splash onto the chrome scissors. The bandage is on my lap and a fresh one is by my side. I can't talk to you or anybody really. My mind is blank and I don't even feel the blade open up the wounds that are already there. I do see the blood though. That part never changes. Seeing red.

Actually, I feel kind of peaceful knowing that the blood is running down over my arm. I'm pressing the point a little deeper so that I feel the sharpness of the blade this time, but the pain somehow becomes a comfort. I'm aware that there is a lot of blood now that I'm cutting deeper, and that it's dripping onto the bed, but I don't care. I'm in a world of my own.

Until there's a scream from downstairs. Mom! The shock makes me slice the blade in deeper, but I soon drop it. I'm only half aware that the blood is spurting from my arm as I jump off the bed and race for the stairs.

When I get to the living room, I stop dead in my tracks. Madeleine is lying on the couch crying and holding her stomach. Her knees are tucked up, but it doesn't stop me from seeing that her pajamas are absolutely soaked with a dark red stain that seems to be growing between her legs. Mom is holding the phone and punching in numbers—calling an ambulance I'm guessing.

"Maddie?"

I can barely get her name out. I'm scared. I notice Mom turn at the sound of my voice.

"Tom?"

I can see that she's not looking at me, but at my arm. I look down and I see that blood is pulsing from an open wound where I'd pushed the scissors too deep.

"Mom…"

I look at Madeleine again and she's crying and hurting and I swear that the blood stain between her legs is getting bigger. And I look to where my own blood is dripping onto the polished wooden floor. And before you know it, I'm sliding down to join it.

CHAPTER 17

New shoes

Well, as you can see, it didn't all end in death and destruction. This is a nice place, I guess. I don't have to do much of anything, and the doctors are kind and they seem to care. I've fallen in love with the nurses, of course. How could I not? They're all so sweet and they seem to make a special fuss over me. Some of them even come to sit with me on their break and we sit and talk and look out over the lawns and the trees in the garden.

Madeleine is coming to see me today. She's coming on her own for the first time. Usually she's with Mom, and to be honest I love seeing both of them. Mom has been really wonderful, and so has Dad, really, but I don't see much of him. He can't just leave his work as easily as Mom can, after all. But I'm really excited that Madeleine is coming alone. I've really missed having special quality time with my sister. Especially since she *has* forgiven me for not being a good enough brother when she needed me most.

Thankfully, Madeleine's bleeding wasn't serious. Well, it was, but because Mom was there to call the ambulance quickly, it was easily resolved. And to be fair, some judicious stitching stemmed the flow of blood from my arm with no problem.

The bandages are still on my arm, as you can see, but it doesn't hurt. The bandages will be off before I leave here. I'm only going to be here for a month. And actually, I don't mind being here, if you must know. For a rehab clinic, it's quite a comfortable hotel, as I constantly tell the nurses. The psychologist I see every day seems happy enough with our little chats. Madeleine and Mom come often, and I've already mentioned how I feel about the nurses, right?

My only dark moments come when I think of Sylvia. And I still think of Sylvia often, particularly late at night in my room when I'm alone. Thinking of Sylvia still hurts more than the cuts on my arm ever could. I'm still in love with Sylvia truth be told, and I go over in my mind how I'll try to win her back after I leave here. In my dreams it's all smooth and easy, but in truth I'm scared. All the same, I *will* try to contact her.

And it's when I think of Sylvia that I believe that I can feel the scar on my arm, carved into the shape of the letter "S," begin to throb. It's a fanciful notion, but real enough to me just the same. And in the darkest moments, I still feel as though I'd like to find some scissors and run the sharp blade points against my skin. I've realized that it's like an addiction. The shrink tells me that I can break that addiction, but something tells me that it won't be easy. I'm always going to have to be on my guard.

I'm wondering what Eddie and everyone at school will say about all this. I guess they'll all have me pegged as a Looney-tune, but what do I care? If I can get back together with Sylvia, they can all say whatever they like. And if we don't get back together, then I'll always have Mom and Madeleine. And the nurses here swear to me that there'll be plenty of other girls—as if girls are all I'm interested in—and like going out with girls will stop me thinking about the scars on my arm and the blades of sharp chrome scissors. Like I'm totally shallow or something.

But then hell, who am I kidding? Maybe the nurses are right. I might think darkly of sharp cold blades from time to time, but I *am* a teenage boy. Of course girls are all I'm interested in. And Madeleine will be here soon with the latest clothes catalogs and the new shoes she's just bought herself. And faced with that prospect, the very last thing I'm going to be thinking of today is seeing red. That can wait for another time.